Disney

FROZEN

ADVENTURES

Ice and Magic

DARK HORSE BOOKS

DARK HORSE BOOKS

PRESIDENT AND PUBLISHER
MIKE RICHARDSON

COLLECTION EDITOR
FREDDYE MILLER

COLLECTION ASSISTANT EDITOR
JUDY KHUU

DESIGNER
BRENNAN THOME

DIGITAL ART TECHNICIAN
SAMANTHA HUMMER

Neil Hankerson Executive Vice President **Tom Weddle** Chief Financial Officer **Randy Stradley** Vice President of Publishing **Nick McWhorter** Chief Business Development Officer **Dale LaFountain** Chief Information Officer **Matt Parkinson** Vice President of Marketing **Cara Niece** Vice President of Production and Scheduling **Mark Bernardi** Vice President of Book Trade and Digital Sales **Ken Lizzi** General Counsel **Dave Marshall** Editor in Chief **Davey Estrada** Editorial Director **Chris Warner** Senior Books Editor **Cary Grazzini** Director of Specialty Projects **Lia Ribacchi** Art Director **Vanessa Todd-Holmes** Director of Print Purchasing **Matt Dryer** Director of Digital Art and Prepress **Michael Gombos** Senior Director of International Publishing and Licensing **Kari Yadro** Director of Custom Programs **Kari Torson** Director of International Licensing **Sean Brice** Director of Trade Sales

DISNEY PUBLISHING WORLDWIDE GLOBAL MAGAZINES, COMICS AND PARTWORKS

PUBLISHER **Lynn Waggoner** • EDITORIAL TEAM **Bianca Coletti** (Director, Magazines), **Guido Frazzini** (Director, Comics), **Carlotta Quattrocolo** (Executive Editor), **Stefano Ambrosio** (Executive Editor, New IP), **Camilla Vedove** (Senior Manager, Editorial Development), **Behnoosh Khalili** (Senior Editor), **Julie Dorris** (Senior Editor), **Mina Riazi** (Assistant Editor), **Gabriela Capasso** (Assistant Editor) • DESIGN **Enrico Soave** (Senior Designer) • ART **Ken Shue** (VP, Global Art), **Manny Mederos** (Senior Illustration Manager, Comics and Magazines), **Roberto Santillo** (Creative Director), **Marco Ghiglione** (Creative Manager), **Stefano Attardi** (Illustration Manager) • PORTFOLIO MANAGEMENT **Olivia Ciancarelli** (Director) • BUSINESS & MARKETING **Mariantonietta Galla** (Senior Manager, Franchise), **Virpi Korhonen** (Editorial Manager)

FROZEN ADVENTURES: ICE AND MAGIC

Published by Dark Horse Books
A division of Dark Horse Comics LLC
10956 SE Main Street, Milwaukie, OR 97222

DarkHorse.com

To find a comics shop in your area, visit comicshoplocator.com

First edition: June 2020 | ISBN 978-1-50671-472-1
Digital ISBN 978-1-50671-475-2

10 9 8 7 6 5 4 3 2 1
Printed in China

This Land Is Our Land

ELSA, THIS IS SOOO EXCITING...

...I'VE ALWAYS WANTED TO GO TO THE LUTEFISK FESTIVAL, I'VE HEARD SO MUCH ABOUT IT!

I DIDN'T THINK YOU WERE VERY FOND OF LUTEFISK, ANNA.

YOU KNOW, I'VE NEVER ACTUALLY TRIED IT...

Script: Georgia Ball; Layouts: Benedetta Barone; Inks: Michela Cacciatore, Rosa La Barbera;
Colors: Kat Maximenko, Jackie Lee, Manuela Nerolini, Sara Spano, Luca Merli, Anastasiia Beloushova, Yana Chinstova; Letters: AndWorld Design

I'VE ALWAYS THOUGHT LUTEFISK SMELLED A LITTLE... FUNNY.
OOO! LUTEFISK FUDGE!
LUTEFISK

DOES THAT ACTUALLY TASTE LIKE...?
PFFT! NO. IT'S JUST SHAPED LIKE A FISH.
WE SHOULD TRY SOME.

LET'S GO THIS WAY!
ANNA, WAIT FOR ME!
PLEASE TAKE SOME, QUEEN ELSA!
IT LOOKS DELICIOUS...

OOO, WHAT'S THIS?
WOULD YOU LIKE TO GIVE IT A GO? JUST THROW THE BALL AS HARD AS YOU CAN TO WIN A PRIZE!

YIKES!
SHOOOP

THAT WAS THE BEST GAME EVER! CAN I DO IT AGAIN?
IF YOU LIKE, OLAF BUT...LET'S GO SEE THE GAMES AT THE OTHER BOOTHS FIRST.
A few minutes later...
THANK YOU, QUEEN ELSA!
COME BACK SOON!
QIVIUT BLANKETS!
SO WARM...
MADE FROM PURE MUSK OX WOOL, SOFTEST IN THE WORLD AND LIGHT AS A FEATHER!
...THEY'RE LOVELY. DO YOU HAVE ANY MORE IN THIS COLOR?
THIS IS THE LAST ONE.
AND MAYBE FOR QUITE A WHILE, IF WE DON'T HAVE ENOUGH GRASSLAND FOR HEALTHY MUSK OX COATS NEXT SEASON.
THERE'S A RUMOR GOING 'ROUND THAT THE REINDEER HERDS WILL BE CROSSING OUR LAND ANY DAY NOW.

THEY'RE CROSSING OUR FARMS TO GET TO THE TUNDRA--
--OH, THOSE BIG, CLOMPING HOOVES, MUDDYING UP THE LAND, EATING UP ALL THE GRASS-- DISGRACEFUL!

BUT THE REINDEER HERDS ALWAYS MIGRATE INLAND FOR THE WINTER. DOESN'T THIS HAPPEN EVERY YEAR?
IT'S NEVER HAPPENED BEFORE! THE HERDERS USUALLY TAKE KRISTTORN PASS.
I SIMPLY DON'T UNDERSTAND IT...

Meanwhile...
HOW MANY OF THESE PILLOWS DO YOU REALLY NEED?
HOW MANY CAN YOU CARRY?

KRISTOFF, LOOK. THIS ONE WILL FIT YOU PERFECTLY!
UM...

I'M GOING TO GET YOU A PRESENT! CLOSE YOUR EYES.
...ALL RIGHT--

SURPRISE!
--OH!

EXCUSE ME--ER...
YES?
...I NEED COUNSEL FROM PRINCESS--UH...
...IS THAT A CARP ON YOUR HEAD?

LOOKS MORE LIKE A SALMON TO ME.
WHAT CAN I DO FOR YOU?
MY APOLOGIES FOR DISTURBING YOU, PRINCESS ANNA. I AM ERET, A REINDEER HERDER. THE REST OF THE REINDEER HERDERS HAVE ASKED ME TO FIND YOU AND SPEAK FOR US ALL.

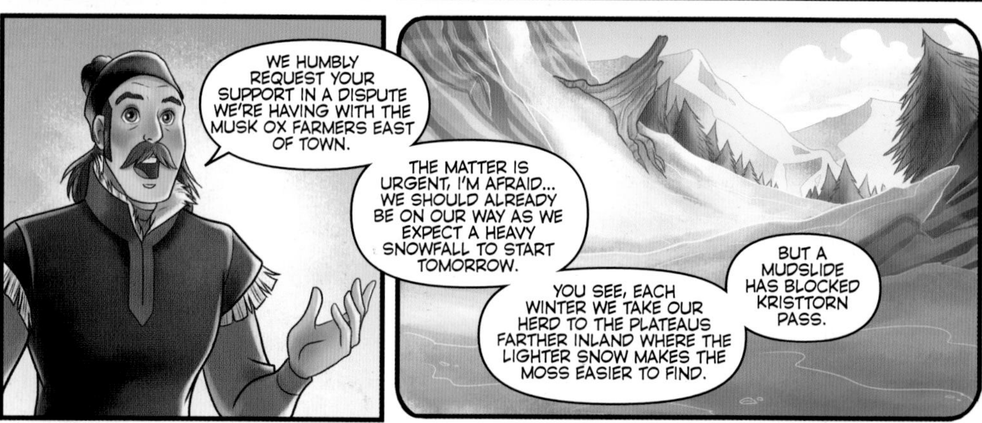
WE HUMBLY REQUEST YOUR SUPPORT IN A DISPUTE WE'RE HAVING WITH THE MUSK OX FARMERS EAST OF TOWN.
THE MATTER IS URGENT, I'M AFRAID... WE SHOULD ALREADY BE ON OUR WAY AS WE EXPECT A HEAVY SNOWFALL TO START TOMORROW.
YOU SEE, EACH WINTER WE TAKE OUR HERD TO THE PLATEAUS FARTHER INLAND WHERE THE LIGHTER SNOW MAKES THE MOSS EASIER TO FIND.
BUT A MUDSLIDE HAS BLOCKED KRISTTORN PASS.

WE MUST CROSS THE FARMERS' PASTURES INSTEAD. THEY'RE ANGRY WITH US BUT WE HAVE NO CHOICE.
WE'VE TRIED TO EXPLAIN BUT THEY WON'T STOP SHOUTING LONG ENOUGH TO LISTEN. MANY OF THEM ARE BUSY WITH THE FESTIVAL TODAY AND THERE'S NO MORE TIME TO ARGUE.

HOW TERRIBLE! I'M SURE QUEEN ELSA WILL HELP.
WE HAVE TO ACT QUICKLY.

WHY IS THIS SO URGENT, KRISTOFF?
IF THE REINDEER DON'T GO EAST BEFORE THE HEAVY SNOWS THEY WON'T HAVE ENOUGH FOOD TO MAKE IT THROUGH THE WINTER.

THE HERDERS' LIVELIHOOD IS AT STAKE, AND THE BAD WEATHER TOMORROW MIGHT DELAY THEM FOR DAYS.
I SEE...

I GREW UP WITH REINDEER, ANNA. SVEN AND I DID EVERYTHING TOGETHER, SO I KNOW HOW IMPORTANT REINDEER ARE TO THEIR HERDERS.
PLEASE TELL ELSA WHAT ERET CAME TO SAY.

WOULD IT BE ALL RIGHT IF I CAME ALONG? I CAN HELP YOU GUIDE THE REINDEER ACROSS THE FIELDS QUICKLY.
WE WOULD BE PLEASED TO HAVE YOU.

BUT IF WE WANT TO AVOID THE SNOW, WE MUST START NOW.
I'LL GET SVEN.
AND I'LL FIND ELSA RIGHT AWAY!

ELSA!
THERE YOU ARE, ANNA! WHERE'S KRISTOFF?

HE'S GONE TO HELP THE REINDEER HERDERS CROSS THE MUSK OX PASTURES!
BUT I JUST PROMISED THE MUSK OX FARMERS I WOULDN'T LET THAT HAPPEN WITHOUT MEETING WITH THE HERDERS FIRST!

OH NO...WHAT SHOULD WE DO?
WE'VE GOT TO REACH THEM-- HURRY!

"BEFORE THINGS GET ANY MORE OUT OF HAND..."

STOP RIGHT THERE.

PLEASE LET US PASS! I PROMISE WE'LL GO THROUGH AS QUICKLY AS WE CAN--
NEVER MIND, KRISTOFF. I'LL TAKE CARE OF THIS.

I KNEW YOU WOULD TRY TO STAND IN OUR WAY, ØRGER.
BUT HERE YOU ARE ALL THE SAME, ERET!

I'M NOT LETTING YOUR HERD DISTURB A BLADE OF GRASS ON MUSK OX LAND.
IS THAT SO? WELL...
...TRY TO STOP US.

I THINK I SEE THEM!
KALLOP KALLOP KALLOP KALLOP

THERE!

THE HERDERS ARE FORCING THEIR WAY THROUGH!
KRISTOFF! YOO-HOO! UP HERE!
I'M AFRAID THE FARMERS MAY NOT LET THEM BY SO EASILY...

I UNDERSTAND HOW KRISTOFF FEELS. THIS IS THE ONLY ROUTE THE HERDERS CAN TAKE!

I UNDERSTAND TOO, ANNA.
BUT A HERD THIS LARGE WILL EAT A LOT OF GRASS ALONG THE WAY.
AND I PROMISED I WOULD PROTECT EVERYONE.

WE NEED TO FIND A WAY TO BRING BOTH SIDES TO AGREEMENT BEFORE SOMEONE GETS HURT.
I'M RIGHT BEHIND YOU, ELSA.
AND I'M BEHIND EVERYBODY!

DO THEY THINK WE'RE JUST GOING TO LET THEM WALK ALL OVER US?

DROP THE STONES TO BLOCK THEIR WAY!

DROP THE STONES TO BLOCK THEIR WAY!

LOOK!

DID YOU HEAR SOMETHING FALL?

GRRR
SEND IN THE DOGS!

RUFF RUFF
RRR RUFF
RUFF

BUH?
RRR RUFF RUFF

SHOOOOSH

ELSA...
HER ICE WALL IS KEEPING THE HERD FROM RUNNING AWAY!

NICE DOGGIE...
HERE BOY!

THE QUEEN IS ON OUR SIDE! KEEP MOVING.

TIME FOR DRASTIC MEASURES.

HEDDY SAID QUEEN ELSA PROMISED TO HELP US AND THIS IS WHAT WE GET???

RELEASE...

...THE CARROT SACKS!
CLOMP CLOMP CLOMP
CLOMP CLOMP

GRUNT GRUNT GRUNT

SVEN! CALL THE REINDEER!

MAAAAWWWWWKRKRKRR

ENOUGH OF THIS. FOLLOW ME.

IT LOOKS LIKE WE'RE FINALLY GETTING A MEETING.

WAIT!

ERET! WE NEED TO TALK THIS THROUGH.
I DON'T FEEL MUCH LIKE TALKING AFTER ALL THE DIRTY TRICKS THE FARMERS PLAYED ON US.

YOU COULD HAVE HURT SOMEONE, ØRGER.
WE WOULDN'T HAVE DONE IT IF THEY HADN'T BARRELED THROUGH OUR LAND WITHOUT OUR CONSENT.

ALL OF US ARE PART OF ARENDELLE, AND WE ALL RELY ON EACH OTHER. I'M SURE THERE'S SOMETHING YOU APPRECIATE ABOUT THE REINDEER HERDERS...
WELL...
MY FAMILY IS RATHER FOND OF REINDEER CHEESE.
SO IS MINE!
WE BUY SOME EVERY TIME WE GO TO MARKET.

AND DON'T YOU DEPEND ON THE MUSK OX FARMERS AS WELL?
WELL...

...QIVIUT YARN DOES MAKE THE BEST WOOL IN ARENDELLE.
I COULD USE A NEW HAT MYSELF.

SEE? YOU NEED EACH OTHER.
PERHAPS THERE'S A WAY EACH OF YOU COULD COMPENSATE THE OTHER?
IN THE MEANTIME...

...NOW YOU CAN CROSS OVER THE PASTURES WITHOUT DAMAGING THE FARMERS' LAND!

I'M SORRY, ØRGER. WILL A FEW WHEELS OF CHEESE MAKE UP FOR ALL THE TROUBLE WE CAUSED YOU?
I DO REALLY LIKE CHEESE.

BUT YOU DID SET YOUR DOGS ON THEM, ØRGER.
THAT WASN'T A VERY NICE THING TO DO, GRANTED.

PLEASE ACCEPT THESE BLANKETS AS A TOKEN OF OUR GOOD WILL!

AND WHEN SPRING COMES AROUND, WE'LL ALL WORK TOGETHER TO CLEAR UP KRISTTORN PASS.
IT WILL BE A PLEASURE.

THE HERD IS ON ITS WAY TO THEIR WINTER HOME AND EVERYTHING WILL BE BACK TO NORMAL SOON, HEDDY.
NEIGHBORS HELPING NEIGHBORS, JUST AS IT SHOULD BE!
AND IN HONOR OF OUR REAFFIRMED FRIENDSHIP, I THINK IT'S TIME--
--THAT WE FINALLY TRY LUTEFISK!
WELL, I THINK WE ALL CAN AGREE ON AT LEAST ONE THING--
--LUTEFISK IS AN ACQUIRED TASTE.
The End

FESTIVE BREAKFAST

Manuscript: Tea Orsi; Layout: Emilio Urbano; Cleanup: Nicoletta Baldari; Color: Stefania Santi

The End

ICE SURPRISE

Manuscript: Alessandro Ferrari; Layout: Elisabetta Melaranci; Cleanup: Rosa la Barbera; Color: Greta Grippa

A Creative Delivery

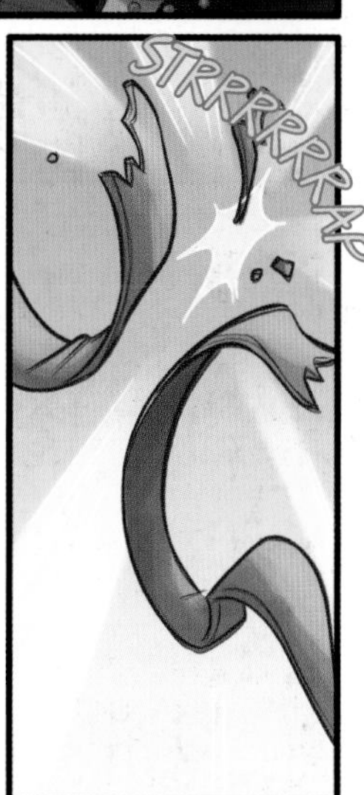

Manuscript: Tea Orsi; Layout: Alberto Zanon; Cleanup: Manuela Razzi; Color: MichelAngela word

AND...
OH NO! I GUESS WE'LL HAVE TO **PUSH** THE SLEIGH TO THE TRADING POST!
OR MAYBE NOT... I HAVE AN **IDEA**!

LEAVE IT TO **ME**!

AFTER SOME QUICK BUT ARTFUL WORK...

IT **WORKS**! AND SVEN SEEMS TO **LOVE** IT TOO!
YES! THESE **ARTCRAFT REINS** ARE A GREAT IDEA!

AND I GUESS OAKEN WILL HAVE ANOTHER GOOD ONE!
2x1
SPECIAL REINS, BUY 2 FOR 1!

The End

To the Rescue!

Script: Tea Orsi; Layout: Marino Gentile; Cleanup: Marino Gentile; Ink: Cristina Stella; Color: Stefania Santi

WHERE COULD IT BE?
I THINK IT'S **THERE!**

HOW SWEET!
CHIRP!
POOR THING! IT LOOKS SO **SCARED!**

DON'T WORRY LITTLE ONE! WE WILL HELP YOU.
WHERE IS ITS **MOTHER?!?**

UHM...MAYBE SHE'S AWAY LOOKING FOR FOOD!

MAYBE THAT'S ITS NEST UP THERE!
OOOH, IT'S WAY UP HIGH!

WE SHOULD TAKE IT BACK TO ITS NEST!
YEAH! I'LL CLIMB UP THERE.

STAY HERE, LITTLE BIRD. I NEED BOTH HANDS.

BUT...
WHEN I GET TO THE TOP, HAND THE BIRD TO ME.
ERM... THAT'S REALLY HIGH, ANNA.
WAIT! I HAVE AN IDEA!

TELL US!
I WANT TO KNOW!
WAIT AND YOU'LL SEE!
AND...
WE NEED A LADDER!
SWISH
WHOA!
NOW YOU CAN CARRY THE BIRD TO THE NEST!
HOW SWEET! THE BABY BIRD LOOKS VERY COZY ON YOUR HEAD, SVEN.

I'M SORRY, BUT IT'S TIME TO GO...

TAKE CARE, LITTLE BIRD!
WE'LL MISS YOU!

THERE IT IS!

IT SEEMS THE BABY BIRD HAS A **TWIN BROTHER**. HELLO, THERE!
CHIRP CHIRP

HERE YOU GO! BACK TOGETHER!
CHIRP CHIRP

SOON, ELSA IS BACK TO THE GROUND...
WILL HE BE OK?
YEAH, NOW IT'S HAPPY AND SAFE WITH ITS BROTHER.

CHIRP
CHIRP
LOOK! ITS MOMMY IS BACK TOO!
JUST IN TIME!

YOU ARE AN AMAZING RESCUER, ELSA!
WHEN SVEN AND I COME BACK TO VISIT THE FAMILY, WE'LL NEED A NEW LADDER.
ERM...

MAYBE WHEN THEY LEARN TO FLY THEY CAN COME SAY HI TO US!
CREEEAK

The End

A Purple Heather!

Manuscript: Tea Orsi; Layout and Cleanup: Elisabetta Melaranci; Color: Dario Calabria

The End

MELTING GIFT

Manuscript: Tea Orsi; Layout: Emilio Urbano; Cleanup: Miriam Gambino; Color: Dario Calabria

The End

THE SEED-OFF CONTEST

ANNA IS VISITING ARENDELLE'S FARMERS...

PRINCESS ANNA! HOW NICE TO SEE YOU. WHAT BRINGS YOU TO MY FARM?

Original story: Erica David; Manuscript adaptation: Chantal Pericoli; Layout: Alberto Zanon; Cleanup: Letizia Algeri; Color: MichelAngela World

LOOK, YOUR HIGHNESS. THE SOIL HAS ALREADY BEEN DIVIDED INTO NEAT ROWS **READY** TO BE **SEEDED!**

YOU'VE DONE AN INCREDIBLE AMOUNT OF WORK HERE.

PRINCESS ANNA!

DID YOU SEE HOW VAST OUR FIELD IS? AND I'VE ALREADY PLANTED **TWO SACKS** OF SEEDS!

I BET YOU'RE THE **FASTEST** IN THE FAMILY.
YES... YAAAWN!
LARS!

OOPS! SORRY.
HAHAHA! DON'T WORRY. WITH ALL THAT PLANTING YOU MUST BE **TIRED**.

WHAT TIME DID YOU GET UP THIS MORNING?

WE USUALLY GET UP AT DAWN AND START WORKING RIGHT AFTER THE FAMILY HAS BREAKFAST.
TODAY WE HAD SMOKED SALMON! YUM!

BUT... WHEN DO YOU PLAY?

WE DON'T MIND. THE FAMILY NEEDS US, AND SO DOES THE TOWN.
AND ANY TIME WE SPEND WITH OUR FAMILY IS A GOOD TIME!

HMMM... IS THERE ANYTHING I CAN DO TO HELP?
OH NO, YOUR HIGHNESS. I WOULDN'T HEAR OF IT!
THIS IS OUR TASK, PRINCESS ANNA.

SEEDING REQUIRES GREAT EXPERTISE. I DON'T KNOW IF YOU'RE ABLE TO DO IT.

YOU WON'T LET ME HELP, EH? WELL, SUPPOSE I CHALLENGE YOU TWO TO A LITTLE SEED-OFF?
WHAT'S A SEED-OFF?

IT'S WHEN WE SEE WHO CAN PLANT THESE ROWS THE FASTEST.

ON YOUR MARK... GET SET...

GO!

SEE?! I'M PRETTY FAST!

BUT WE'RE FASTER!

ALMOST FINISHED...

I WON!

CONGRATULATIONS! YOU'RE THE WINNER OF THE FIRST OFFICIAL MULLENER FARM SEED-OFF!

MOM! DAD! I WON!

NOW IT'S TIME TO PLAY!

SO YOU TRICKED THEM INTO LETTING YOU HELP.
EVERYONE CAN USE A LITTLE HELP NOW AND THEN... EVEN FROM A PRINCESS! HAHAHA!

The End

THE PERFECT GAME

TOMORROW ANNA AND ELSA ARE HOSTING THE TOWNSPEOPLE FOR THE TRADITIONAL WINTER PARTY...

NO, NO. THIS WON'T WORK, EITHER!

ELSA, YOU SEEM SO STRESSED. WHAT'S TROUBLING YOU?

Original story by Erica David; Adapted by Tea Orsi; Layout: GAlberto Zanon; Clean: Nicoletta Baldari; Color: Dario Calabria

WHAT DID YOU WANT TO SHOW ME?
NOTHING! I JUST THOUGHT THAT YOU NEEDED A **REFRESHING BREAK** TO FIND THE RIGHT IDEA, SO...

SPLAT

...WHAT'S BETTER THAN **SNOWBALLS**?

A DUEL THEN?!
MAY THE BEST WIN!

SWOOOSH
HAHA! TRY AGAIN!

SOON OLAF AND KRISTOFF JOIN THE SISTERS...

SWISH

SWOSH

THIS IS JUST LIKE WHEN WE WERE KIDS!

THAT'S RIGHT! WE WOULD PLAY LIKE THIS EVERY WINTER.

THE NEXT DAY, AT THE WINTER PARTY...
SWOOSH
SPLAT
SWISH
IT LOOKS LIKE YOU DIDN'T NEED TO WORRY ABOUT ORIGINALITY AND TRADITION AFTER ALL...
YES, WHEN YOU'RE WITH FRIENDS EVEN THE SIMPLEST ACTIVITY IS UNIQUE!
AND NOW... HOW ABOUT WE JOIN IN THE FUN?
I THOUGHT YOU'D NEVER ASK!

The End

A NEW REINDEER FRIEND

Manuscript: Alessandro Ferrari; Layout: Elisabetta Melaranci;
Cleanup: Veronica Di Lorenzo; Paint: Dario Calabria and Silvano Scolari

A MOMENT LATER ANNA, ELSA AND OLAF ARE WALKING IN THE MOUNTAIN FIELDS TO FIND CROCUSES...
I LOVE CROCUSES!

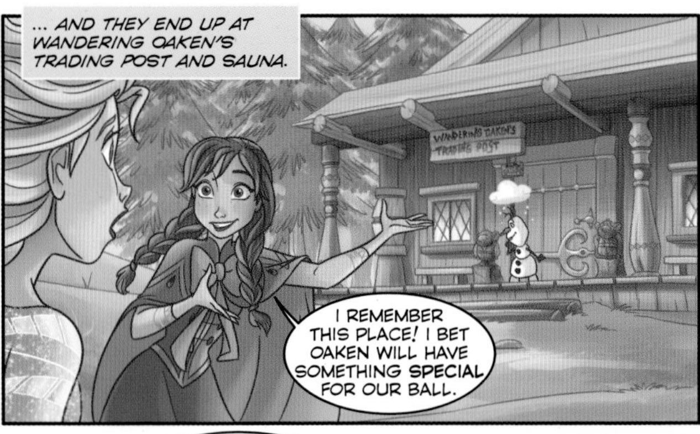
... AND THEY END UP AT WANDERING OAKEN'S TRADING POST AND SAUNA.
I REMEMBER THIS PLACE! I BET OAKEN WILL HAVE SOMETHING **SPECIAL** FOR OUR BALL.

HOO HOO! MY BIG WINTER BLOWOUT IS SPECIAL!
HALF OFF SHOES FOR WALKING ON SNOW AND KARTS FOR SLIDING DOWN MOUNTAINS!

SEE? I TOLD YOU!
THIS IS THE **BEST DAY** OF MY LIFE! I CAN'T WAIT TO FIND LOTS OF...
GASP!

THE CROCUSES!
THEY'RE BEAUTIFUL!

LOOK AT ME... I'M A **GARDEN**!

ANNA AND ELSA ARE STILL COLLECTING CROCUSES WHEN...

...OLAF STARTS CHASING A LITTLE BEE...
HIHIHI! COME HERE!

I BET YOU LIKE **HUGS** AS MUCH AS I...

...WHOOPS!

HOW DID IT GET DOWN THERE? AND HOW ARE WE GOING TO SAVE IT?

WE HAVE TO HELP IT...

fwhooo
FIRST, WE NEED A RAMP...

...SECOND, I SLIDE DOWN!

I KNEW THESE WOULD BE USEFUL...
?

ANNA, ELSA AND OLAF MANAGE TO SAVE THE LITTLE REINDEER BY WORKING TOGETHER...

...AND THE YOUNG REINDEER IMMEDIATELY BECOMES THEIR FRIEND!
CAN WE INVITE HIM TO THE BALL?

THE BALL! WE'LL BE LATE!
fshh
DON'T WORRY, ANNA...

"...WE JUST NEED SOME MAGIC!"
ARE YOU READY?
I'M OLAF, BUT I CAN BE READY TOO.

FASTEEEEER!
WHOOO

SLIDING ON ELSA'S MAGIC RAMP...
WHOOO

... THE GROUP GETS TO ARENDELLE IN NO TIME AT ALL...
ALMOST THERE!

... AND LANDS IN THE MIDDLE OF THE BALLROOM WITH THE BEST GRAND ENTRANCE EVER SEEN!
HERE WE ARE!
ALL TOGETHER!
AND WITH A NEW FRIEND!
FINALLY, THE BALL CAN BEGIN...

The End

Reach for the Lights

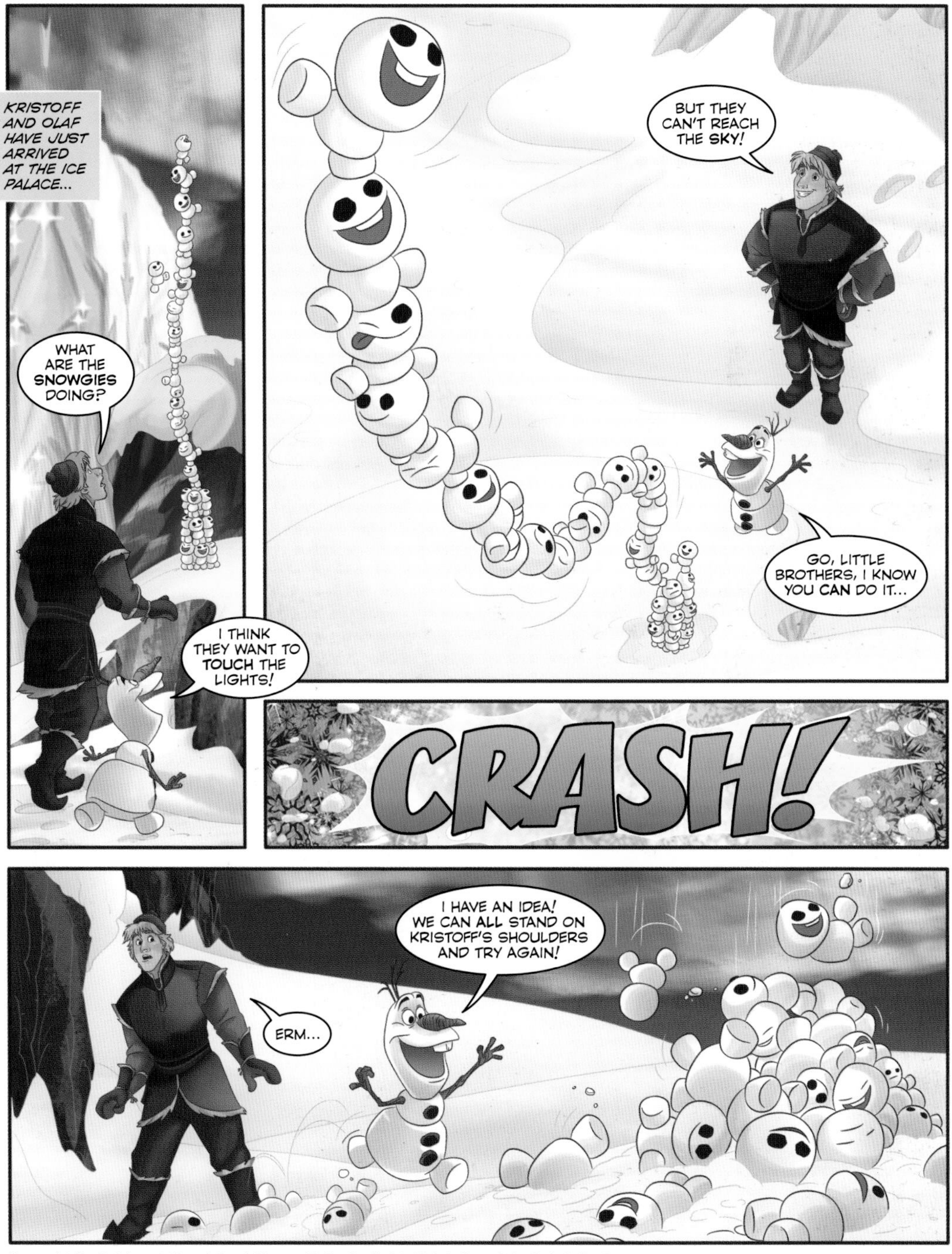

KRISTOFF AND OLAF HAVE JUST ARRIVED AT THE ICE PALACE...

WHAT ARE THE **SNOWGIES** DOING?

I THINK THEY WANT TO **TOUCH** THE LIGHTS!

BUT THEY **CAN'T** REACH THE **SKY**!

GO, LITTLE BROTHERS, I KNOW YOU **CAN** DO IT...

CRASH!

Manuscript: Tea Orsi; Layout: Manuela Razzi; Cleanup: Marino Gentile; Ink: Michela Frare; Color: Stefania Santi

The End

SWEET TRICK

Manuscript: Alessandro Ferrari; Layout: Elisabetta Melaranci; Cleanup: Arianna Rea, Federica Salfo; Ink: Michela Frare, Cristina Stella; Color: Dario Calabria

The End

A Day On The Beach

Manuscript: Tea Orsi; Layout: Alberto Zanon; Cleanup: Veronica Di Lorenzo; Color: Manuela Nerolini

AND, WHEN THEY GET TO THE BEACH...
SWISH
I LOVE THE FEELING OF SAND ON MY SNOW! WHY DON'T YOU TRY?
I'D ACTUALLY PREFER SOME SNOW ON THE SAND!
MAYBE LATER, OLAF!
THE FUN GOES ON, BUT...
IT LOOKS LIKE ME!
LUCKILY YOUR SNOW CLOUD IS BIG ENOUGH TO KEEP YOU COOL IN THE SUN, OLAF!
IT SURELY IS! BUT MAYBE WE NEED ONE, TOO...
GOOD IDEA!
NOW WE WILL ENJOY THIS SUMMER DAY EVEN MORE!
SUMMER IS JUST AMAZING!
The End

DRAGON DAYS!

IT'S THE PERFECT DAY FOR A WALK IN THE FORESTS OF ARENDELLE!

I LOVE THE FOREST!

YOU DO?

WHY'S THAT?

Adapted from *Anna & Elsa: The Secret Admirer* written by Erica David; Manuscript adaptation by: Steve Behling; Layout: Marino Gentile; Clean: Marino Gentile; Ink and Color: MAAWillustration

STAY HERE--I'LL INVESTIGATE!
OLAF...

CRASH
MAYBE IT'S MARSHMALLOW, JUST HAVING SOME FUN!

OR KRISTOFF, DROPPING A GIANT STACK OF POTS AND PANS BECAUSE HE'S CLUMSY!
CLANK
CRASH

SINCE WHEN DOES KRISTOFF CARRY AROUND POTS AND PANS?
SINCE WHEN IS KRISTOFF CLUMSY?

HMMMM...

THEN MAYBE IT'S A BAND! BANGING CYMBALS TOGETHER! THEY'RE FAR AWAY ON THE MOUNTAIN AND THE ECHOES TRAVEL A GIGANTIC DISTANCE!

I DON'T THINK SO, OLAF. LET'S SEE WHAT IS MAKING THOSE SOUNDS...

CLANK
MORE LIKE "WHO!"

IT'S A LITTLE BOY WITH A PRETEND SWORD!
CLANK

TAKE THAT! AND THAT!

DON'T WORRY, MY QUEEN--WE'LL SAVE THE VILLAGE TOGETHER!

REMIND YOU OF ANYONE, ELSA?
US--WE PLAYED GAMES LIKE THAT WHEN WE WERE LITTLE!
WHAT DO YOU SAY, WE GIVE HIM A SURPRISE?
I SAY...YES!
I SAY YES, TOO! I LIKE SAYING YES!
WHAT DID YOU HAVE IN MIND?
A LITTLE SOMETHING...
...LIKE...
...THIS!
THAT'S PERFECT!
EEEEP!

NOW, TO GET HIS ATTENTION...
AHEM!
HUH? WHAT'S THAT SOUND?
A DRAGON! AHHHHHHHHH!!!
UH-OH! I GUESS MY SURPRISE WAS A LITTLE TOO SURPRISING!
SAVE MEEE!

THUMP
Y-YOUR MAJESTY! I'M SORRY!
NO, I'M SORRY I SCARED YOU!

IT'S JUST AN ICE SCULPTURE. I SAW YOU WERE PRETENDING, SO I THOUGHT TO GIVE YOU A PRETEND MONSTER.
AND I WAS SUPPOSED TO BE THE HERO. I GUESS YOU SAVED ME!

THAT'S OKAY! EVERYONE NEEDS A RESCUE SOMETIMES! QUEENS AND PRINCESSES GET TO DO THE RESCUING TOO.
GREAT JOB, ELSA!
I'LL SAY! NOW LET'S GO FIGHT THAT DRAGON!

The End

THE WRONG ROCK

Manuscript: Tea Orsi; Layout: Emilio Urbano; Cleanup: Manuela Razzi; Color: Stefania Santi

The End

OAKEN'S MYSTERY BOX

Manuscript: Tea Orsi; Layout: Alberto Zanon;
Cleanup: Rosa La Barbera; Color: Stefania Santi

Incredible Display

IT'S THE PERFECT DAY TO VISIT OAKEN!

WOW, LOOK AT ALL THE PEOPLE!

YAH, WITH THIS NICE WEATHER...

Manuscript: Tea Orsi; Layout: Federica Salfo; Cleanup: Letizia Algeri; Color: Stefania Santi

BUT...

LOOKS LIKE OAKEN IS **TOO BUSY** TO SET IT UP.

IT'S A PITY! HE HAS SO MANY INVENTIONS TO SHOW.

SO...

THUMP

WOOOSHHH

FINALLY...

... EVERYONE CAN SEE YOUR AMAZING INVENTIONS, NOW. THIS WHEELED MONO-SKI IS SO MUCH FUN!
OAKEN'S INVENTION DISPLAY
BIG SALE TODAY! ALL INVENTIONS TWO FOR ONE! GREAT DEAL, YAH?

The End

GUESTS OF HONOR

Manuscript: Alessandro Ferrari; Layout: Nicoletta Baldari; Cleanup: Federica Salfo; Ink: Michela Frare; Color: Stefania Santi

The End

OLAF'S CLOUD

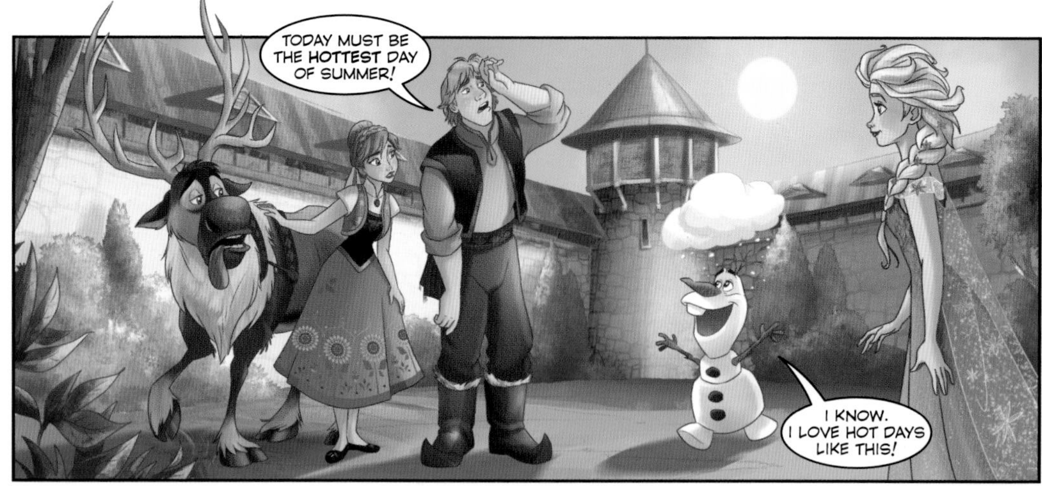

Manuscript: Tea Orsi; Layout: Emilio Urbano; Cleanup: Marino Gentile; Ink: Michela Frare; Color: Dario Calabria

A GREAT NARRATOR

Manuscript: Tea Orsi; Layout: Alberto Zanon; Cleanup: Letizia Algeri; Color: MichelAngela World

LATER, AT THE CASTLE...
THIS IS WHERE HE FOUND THE TREASURE MAP...
?!?

...AND FOLLOWED ITS SECRET PATH...

SWOOSH
...TO FIND THE BEST SNOWY TREASURE EVER!

ARE YOU READY FOR ANOTHER ADVENTURE ON THE MYSTERY ISLAND?
THE SNOWGIES ARE SO CALM AND FOCUSED...
BECAUSE OLAF IS A GREAT NARRATOR!

The End

A Kite for Olaf

Manuscript: Valentina Cambi; Layout: Alberto Zanon; Cleanup: Letizia Algeri; Color: MichelAngela World

WOW!

LOOK UP THERE!

WHAT IS THAT?
IT'S A FLYING TOY CALLED A KITE!
CRUNCH, CRUNCH

I'VE NEVER SEEN SUCH AN EXCITING TOY!

I WISH I COULD HAVE ONE!
ALL RIGHT! EVEN THOUGH WE DON'T HAVE THE RIGHT GEAR TO BUILD A KITE, I CAN TRY!

WE'LL HELP YOU!
YES, THIS WILL BE FUN!
LET'S GET TO WORK, THEN!

WHAT DO YOU THINK OF A NAPKIN AS THE SAIL?
THAT'S A GOOD IDEA!

AND NOW THE FRAME... WE COULD USE SOME TWIGS...

THOSE ARE PERFECT, BUDDY!

WE'RE ALMOST DONE! WE ONLY HAVE TO FIND A THREAD TO FASTEN ALL THE PARTS AND TO HOLD THE KITE...

WHAT ABOUT THE STRINGS OF YOUR LUTE?
MY LUTE???

IT'S FOR A GOOD CAUSE!
YOU CAN ALWAYS BUY NEW STRINGS AT OAKEN'S!
UHM... FINE...

HERE WE ARE!
WHAT A GREAT KITE!
OHHH!!!

HAVE FUN!
THIS IS THE BEST KITE EVER!

I LOVE KITES!

IT FLIES SO HIGH!

THUD

MY ARM IS FLYING!

THAT'S OLAF'S KITE!
AND THAT'S HIS ARM!

WE HAVE TO DO SOMETHING!

I THINK THIS WILL WORK!

FREEZE

IT WORKED!
WELL DONE ELSA!
TUMP

MY ARM!

A FEW MOMENTS LATER...

The End

THE LOST MAP

Manuscript: Tea Orsi; Layout: Nicoletta Baldari; Cleanup: Veronica Di Lorenzo; Color: Stefania Santi

OLAF AND SVEN AGREE TOO, AND...

AFTER A SHORT WALK...

HUH?!?

I KNEW IT!

THIS IS **INCREDIBLE!**

THE THREE PATHS HAVE TAKEN US TO THE **MEADOW** WE WERE LOOKING FOR!

ALL OF US WERE **RIGHT!**

ALL RIGHT... AND **MEANT** TO BE TOGETHER! TEE-HEE!

The End

Dark Lake

Manuscript: Valentina Cambi; Layout: Emilio Urbano; Pencil: Manuela Razzi; Ink/Paint: Michelangela_World

BE CAREFUL, OLAF!
OOPS!

HOW DO THEY WORK?
I'LL SHOW YOU WHEN WE GET THERE!

WE'VE GOTTA GO NOW!

ARE WE IN A HURRY?
YEP! IT GETS DARK EARLY, SO WE DON'T HAVE MUCH TIME!

I SEE...
THE DARK LAKE IS FAR AWAY AND USUALLY NOBODY GOES THERE...BUT IT'S THE PERFECT PLACE TO TEACH YOU.

A FEW HOURS LATER...
WE'VE ARRIVED!
HOW BEAUTIFUL!

KRISTOFF IMMEDIATELY GETS TO WORK.
FIRST WE NEED TO CUT THE ICE!

THEN WE JAB AT THE BLOCK OF ICE UNTIL IT BREAKS THROUGH...

OLAF CAN'T WAIT TO HELP!
...AND FINALLY WE GET IT! LIKE THIS!

BUT ICE HARVESTING IS HARD WORK...
PANT! PANT!

WHOA!!!
SPLASH

COOL!

SLAM

ARE YOU ALL RIGHT, OLAF?
I AM! THAT WAS SO MUCH FUN!

SUDDENLY OLAF NOTICES SOMETHING STRANGE IN THE SNOW...

LOOK! THERE ARE HUGE FOOTPRINTS!

KREEEK
KREEEK
KREEEK

KREEEK
THAT'S A STRANGE NOISE.

UHM... IT'S PROBABLY THE WIND OR...

YOU THINK IT'S A MONSTER, SVEN?
WHAT'S A MONSTER?
A MONSTER IS USUALLY A VERY SCARY CREATURE THAT--

UH?
KREEEK

!!!!

THUD

OH NO!

SPLASH

GRAB IT!

HANG ON TIGHT!

KRISTOFF, I DIDN'T KNOW YOU LIKED SWIMMING SO MUCH!
THANK YOU!

WHO ARE YOU?
I LIVE IN THE WOODS NEARBY AND I WAS OUT TO GATHER SOME FOOD.

ON MY WAY BACK, I HEARD SOME NOISE, SO I CAME BACK TO SEE WHAT IT WAS, AND I SAW YOU!
I LOVE YOUR HAT!...

ALONG THE WAY MY SNOWSHOES BROKE, SO I REPAIRED THEM THE BEST I COULD...
...AND YOUR SHOES, TOO!

KREEEK

HA-HA-HA!
THAT NOISE... THE MONSTER IS BACK! I WANT TO SEE HIM!

The End

DIFFERENT PERSPECTIVES

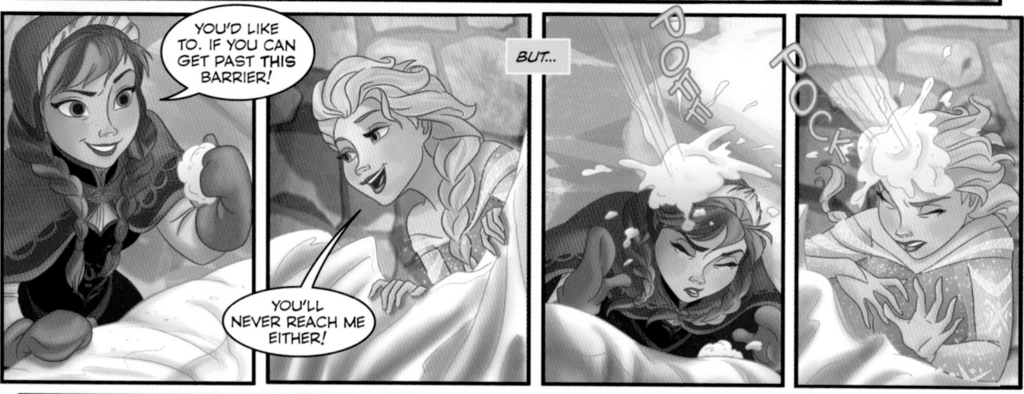

Manuscript: Tea Orsi; Layout: Alberto Zanon; Cleanup: Marino Gentile; Ink: Michela Frare; Color: Stefania Santi

The End

The Icy Playground

"WE HARVESTED A LOT OF ICE, BUT THEN WE STOPPED AT THE ICE PALACE AND..."

SWOOSH

SWISH

SO... WHO IS GONNA TELL THEM THAT WE HAVE TO GO?

Manuscript: Tea Orsi; Layout: Emilio Urbano; Cleanup: Nicoletta Baldari; Color: Alessandra Bracaglia

The Strongest Man in Arendelle!

IMPORTANT AMBASSADORS WILL ARRIVE SOON IN ARENDELLE, AND ANNA HAS AN IDEA TO WELCOME THEM...

I DON'T KNOW, ANNA. THE ICE PALACE WAS NEVER MEANT TO HOST IMPORTANT GUESTS.

Original story: Erica David; Adaptation: Chantal Pericoli; Layout and Cleanup: Benedetta Barone; Color: Dario Calabria

HMM, I GUESS I COULD MAKE IT A LITTLE MORE COMFORTABLE.
WHOOP
WHOOP
WHOOP

I'LL USE MY POWERS TO MAKE FURNITURE OUT OF ICE.

I CAN BE OF ASSISTANCE TOO. AFTER ALL, I AM A PROFESSIONAL ICE HARVESTER. I CAN CARVE ANYTHING OUT OF ICE.

GOOD IDEA. HOW ABOUT A DINING TABLE AND SOME CHAIRS?

NEXT DELIVERY: A DINING TABLE. HAHAH!

GATHER AROUND, LITTLE BROTHERS. THE AMBASSADORS ARE VERY IMPORTANT GUESTS...

AND I KNOW ALL ABOUT WHAT TO DO, OR RATHER, WHAT **NOT** TO DO, WHEN IMPORTANT GUESTS COME TO VISIT...

THE BEST WAY TO MAKE THEM FEEL WELCOME IS TO GREET THEM WITH... **A SURPRISE!**

LET'S PRACTICE: LINE UP, AND WHEN I GIVE THE SIGNAL, YOU JUMP, ONE AFTER THE OTHER, STARTING WITH THE FIRST ONE IN LINE...

THIS WILL LOOK LIKE ONE **BIG WELCOME WAVE!** EVERYBODY READY?

WAIT, NO... DON'T... THAT'S NOT...

AT THE SAME TIME, OUTSIDE THE PALACE...
WOW, THE AMBASSADORS WILL BE ASTONISHED BY THE SPIRES! LOOK HOW THEY GLITTER AGAINST THE SKY.

!!!

POING
POING
WHAT ON EARTH?

PUT ME DOWN! WE'VE GOT WORK TO DO!
SHOULD WE BE WORRIED?
IF I KNOW OLAF, THEY'LL BE BACK IN TIME FOR BED.

FINALLY, THE GREAT EVENING COMES...
WELCOME, AMBASSADORS! PLEASE HAVE A SEAT, EVERYONE!
IS EVERYTHING ALL RIGHT, OLAF?
YES, THE SNOWGIES ARE ALL LINED UP BEHIND THE CURTAIN. **THE WELCOME WAVE** WILL BE FANTASTIC!

TA-DA!

?
BUT... WHERE ARE THE SNOWGIES?
THEY MUST'VE THOUGHT THIS WAS PART OF THEIR FAVORITE GAME, HIDE-AND-SEEK. I GUESS THEY FOUND A NEW HIDING SPOT.

FOLLOW ME, I'VE GOT AN IDEA!

LADIES AND GENTLEMEN, MAY I PRESENT TO YOU **KRISTOFF THE MAGNIFICENT!** THE STRONGEST MAN IN ARENDELLE!
I AM? I MEAN, OF COURSE I AM!

FOR HIS FIRST DISPLAY OF STRENGTH, WATCH AS KRISTOFF LIFTS... OLAF!

DON'T LET OLAF'S APPEARANCE FOOL YOU. HE MAY LOOK AS LIGHT AS A **SNOWFLAKE**, BUT HE'S HEAVIER THAN AN **AVALANCHE**!
CLAP CLAP CLAP

AND NOW... **PRINCESS ANNA**!

!

ACTUALLY... DINNER IS SERVED... WE CAN'T LET OUR FOOD GET COLD!

GREAT IDEA...

BUT NOW WE'LL HAVE TO EXPLAIN WHY A COLD DINNER CAN'T WAIT ANY LONGER!
>GASP!<

The End

Snow School

Manuscript: Alessandro Ferrari; Layout: Elisabetta Melaranci;
Cleanup: Veronica Di Lorenzo; Color: Dario Calabria

...BUILT AN ICE TRACK FOR ALL THE STUDENTS TO SLIDE TO SCHOOL!
FWHOOOSH
GOOOOOO!
FWHOOOSH

I JUST LOVE...

... TO GO TO SCHOOL!

I CAN'T BELIEVE IT.
ME NEITHER. ACTUALLY...

... DO YOU THINK I COULD SLIDE TO THE VILLAGE MARKET, YOUR MAJESTY?
OF COURSE!
FSHHHOOO
The End

The Ice Harvester Fair

Manuscript: Tea Orsi; Layout: Ciro Cangialosi; Pencil: Letizia Algeri; Paint: Dario Calabria

KRISTOFF! IT'S GOOD TO SEE YOU!
I'VE NEVER MET A *TALKING* SNOWMAN!
HI, I'M OLAF AND I LIKE WARM HUGS!

PLEASED TO MEET YA, BUDDY!

HUH?!?
THAT'S OKAY!

I HOPE I'LL ALSO BE THAT STRONG WHEN I PLAY ***TIP THE BARREL!***

WHAT'S TIP THE BARREL, KRISTOFF?
IT'S ONE OF THE MANY ACTIVITIES WE ARE GOING TO PLAY TOMORROW!
WE WHACK A BIG BARREL FULL OF TREATS. THE ONE WHO MAKES IT FALL WINS EVERTHING INSIDE!
"SOUNDS FUN! WHAT ABOUT THE OTHER ACTIVITIES?"
"THERE'S THE SNOW SCULPTURE CONTEST!
"PIN THE TAIL ON THE REINDEER...
"...AND RETRIEVE THE FROZEN APPLE!
"AND FINALLY, THE GREATEST SNOWBALL FIGHT EVER!"

OKAY, IT'S TIME TO SET UP FOR THE FAIR!
I'M READY!

SO... I THINK EVERYBODY IS HERE, RIGHT?
WAIT!

ALBIN HASN'T ARRIVED YET! HE WAS SUPPOSED TO BE HERE BY NOW.
HUH?! YOU'RE RIGHT! I HAVEN'T SEEN HIM!

I HOPE HE'S OKAY.
DON'T WORRY, WE'LL GO LOOK FOR HIM!

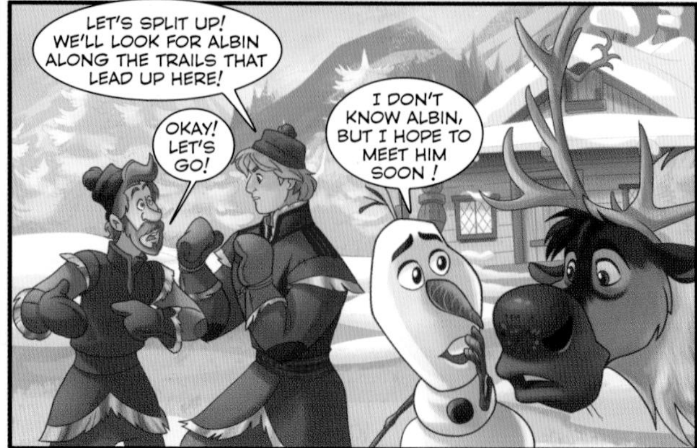
LET'S SPLIT UP! WE'LL LOOK FOR ALBIN ALONG THE TRAILS THAT LEAD UP HERE!
OKAY! LET'S GO!
I DON'T KNOW ALBIN, BUT I HOPE TO MEET HIM SOON !

SEE YOU LATER, FRIENDS!
GO, SVEN! WE'LL TAKE THE PATH THAT RUNS ALONGSIDE THE FOREST!
WOOSH

OH, I LIKE THIS !
IT'S AN EMERGENCY HORN! WE'LL BLOW IT TO CALL THE OTHERS IF WE FIND ALBIN!

HEY, SVEN! WHY DID YOU STOP?
SCREEECH!

MAYBE HE'S LOOKING AT OUR TRACKS!

UHM...THESE ARE NOT OURS! ***ANOTHER SLEIGH*** RODE ON THIS TRAIL EARLIER!

BUT IT VEERED OFF THE TRAIL AND ENTERED THE FOREST. THIS IS STRANGE!

IT MIGHT BE ALBIN! LET'S GO AND SEE!

OUR FRIENDS FOLLOW THE TRACKS AND...
A ***SLEIGH!*** I THINK THAT'S ALBIN'S!
WHERE IS HE? I CAN'T SEE HIM!

I DON'T KNOW, BUT I WANT TO FIND OUT!

HEEEEELP!
HUH?! DID YOU HEAR THAT?
I HEARD IT!

WE'RE COMING! WHERE ARE YOU?
BYE! WE'LL BE BACK SOON!

THE GANG CROSSES THE FOREST, AND...
HELP ME, PLEASE! I CAN'T GET BACK TO THE BANK!
IT'S ALBIN!
AND A PUPPY!

WE'VE GOT TO RESCUE HIM QUICKLY!

SWOOSH
TRY TO CATCH THE ROPE, ALBIN!
SWOOSH

BUT...
OH NO! IT'S TOO SHORT!

GASP!
CRACK

THE ICE IS CRACKING! DON'T MOVE! IT'S TOO DANGEROUS!

THE OTHERS SHOULDN'T BE THAT FAR AWAY. HOPEFULLY THEY'LL HEAR US!

HOOOOOOOOO

LUCKILY, THE SOUND OF THE HORN IS REALLY LOUD.
KRISTOFF! WHAT'S GOING ON?
QUICK! I NEED MORE ROPES AND SOME HELP!

THE HARVESTERS AND OLAF GET TO WORK IMMEDIATELY...
THE KNOTS NEED TO BE VERY STRONG!
THIS ROPE IS BECOMING LONGER AND LONGER...!

...AND...
SWOOSH
...CAUGHT!

HEAVE-HOOOO!
AHHHH!
WOOSH

WE DID IT!
TAKE THIS, BUDDY! YOU MUST BE FREEZING!
HURRAY!

THANK YOU, GUYS! YOU SAVED OUR LIVES!
BUT... WHAT WERE YOU DOING THERE?
YEAH... HOW DID YOU END UP ON THAT PIECE OF ICE?

I BROUGHT MY DOG WITH ME. SOMETHING MUST HAVE CAUGHT HIS ATTENTION, 'CAUSE HE SUDDENLY JUMPED OFF MY SLEIGH AND RAN OFF...

"...I KNEW THERE WAS A CHANCE THE ICE WAS TOO THIN, BUT I COULDN'T LEAVE HIM THERE..."
HUH?!?
CRACK

THE NEXT MORNING, AFTER SOME MUCH NEEDED SLEEP...

WELCOME TO THE FIRST ANNUAL ICE HARVESTER FAIR!

WE HAD A TOUGH DAY YESTERDAY...

BUT EVERYTHING WENT WELL IN THE END! AND NOW WE CAN HAVE FUN TOGETHER !

YEAH! GOOD IDEA!

I LIKE IT!

GREAT! THEN, LET THE FAIR BEGIIIIIIIN!

FINALLY, IT'S TIME FOR SOME SNOW SCULPTURE BUILDING FUN!
THREE... TWO...ONE... GO!

WHAT KIND OF SNOW SCULPTURE CAN I BUILD? ELSA ALWAYS HELPS ME...

WELL...YOU ARE A SNOWMAN! YOU DON'T EVEN NEED TO BUILD A SCULPTURE.
HUH?!? YOU'RE RIGHT!

HEY! ALBIN SAID I'M DONE!
ALREADY?!? HUH? YOU REALLY ARE!
ERM... KRISTOFF, MAYBE NEXT YEAR WE SHOULD COME UP WITH SPECIAL RULES...

...JUST IN CASE YOU HAVE MORE SNOWMAN FRIENDS LIKE HIM TO BRING OVER!
DON'T WORRY, I CAN ASSURE YOU THAT OLAF IS ONE OF A KIND!

The End

ICE SKATING SHOW

Manuscript: Tea Orsi; Layot: Nicoletta Baldari;
Cleanup: Nicoletta Baldari; Color: Stefania Santi

The End

VILLAGE FLOWERS

Manuscript: Tea Orsi; Layout: Alberto Zanon; Cleanup: Marino Gentile; Ink: Michela Frare; Color: MichelAngela World

The End

THE MOST SPECIAL GIFT

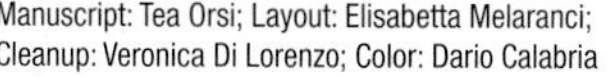

Manuscript: Tea Orsi; Layout: Elisabetta Melaranci;
Cleanup: Veronica Di Lorenzo; Color: Dario Calabria

SEE YA LATER! I PROMISED TO TAKE OLAF ON A LITTLE BOAT TRIP.
HAVE FUN!

ANNA DESERVES A GIFT, TOO!

I'LL MAKE SOMETHING NICE FOR HER!

SHORTLY THEREAFTER...
HERE IT IS! JUST TO LET ANNA KNOW THAT I LOVE HER.
SWISH

BUT...

OH, NO! I DIDN'T CONSIDER THE WARM WEATHER.

UHM...I MUST THINK ABOUT SOMETHING DIFFERENT.

ELSA REACHES THE VILLAGE LOOKING FOR INSPIRATION, AND...

HEY, KRISTOFF!

ELSA?!?

DON'T WORRY, I'LL COME UP WITH A GOOD IDEA!
IF YOU GET A SPARE ONE, LET ME KNOW!
ELSA KNOWS WHO TO ASK...
I NEED YOUR ADVICE!

QUEEN ELSA!
HOW CAN WE HELP YOU?
I'LL TELL YOU IMMEDIATELY!

ELSA EXPLAINS EVERYTHING, AND...
GIVE HER A NEW DRESS!
A BABY REINDEER!
CHOCOLATE COOKIES!

CALM DOWN!
PABBIE!

REMEMBER, THE SIMPLEST THING COULD BE THE MOST WONDERFUL PRESENT.
YOU'RE RIGHT, PABBIE.

WHILE GETTING BACK HOME, ELSA KEEPS THINKING ABOUT PABBIE'S WORDS...
MAYBE THE SIMPLEST THING IS THE HARDEST TO FIND...

BUT ON THE WAY BACK TO THE CASTLE...
!
I LOVE THIS SUMMER SLEIGH.
IT'S CALLED A WAGON! IT'S SO BIG WE CAN ALL RIDE TOGETHER!

I'LL TALK TO KRISTOFF!

NEXT MORNING...
WHERE ARE WE GOING?
IT'S A SURPRISE!

ARE YOU READY FOR A VERY SPECIAL PICNIC TRIP?!
CLIMB ABOARD!
WHOA!

WE'RE GOING TO SPEND A WONDERFUL DAY TOGETHER!
WE SURELY WILL!

DID I TELL YOU THAT YOU'RE THE BEST SISTER EVER?
DID I TELL YOU THAT YOU ARE TOO?

The End

The Happiest Anthem

Original Story: Erica David; Adaptation: Chantal Pericoli; Layout: Gianluca Barone; Clean: Caterina Giorgetti; Color: MichelAngela World

YOU PLAY BEAUTIFULLY!
THANK YOU...

QUEEN ELSA?!?

YOUR MAJESTY, PLEASE ACCEPT THE NEXT SONG AS AN HOMAGE FROM US!
WITH PLEASURE!

THIS ISN'T A SONG... IT'S THE ROYAL ANTHEM.

I THINK THE VILLAGERS PREFER THE OTHER SONGS...
DON'T WORRY, THEY'LL KEEP ON DANCING AFTER THE ANTHEM.

BUT ARENDELLE'S ROYAL ANTHEM ISN'T JUST SLOW... IT IS ALSO LONG!
WHY DON'T WE CLAP ALONG?
GOOD IDEA!

BUT...
IT DOESN'T WORK! THE RHYTHM IS TOO SLOW.
HMMM, LET'S TRY SOMETHING ELSE...

LET'S DANCE!

THE ROYAL ANTHEM HAS NEVER SOUNDED SO GOOD!

AND THIS IS ALL THANKS TO **YOU**, ANNA! HAHAHA!

The End

A Special Teacher

Manuscript: Tea Orsi; Layout: Emilio Urbano;
Cleanup: Manuela Razzi; Color: Patrizia Zangrilli and Luca Merli

HELLO!
PRINCESS ANNA?!?
HI!

CALL ME **ANNA**! WHAT'S YOUR NAME?
I'M **MATHILDE**, YOUR MAJES-- ERM... ANNA!

WHY AREN'T YOU ICE SKATING, MATHILDE?
BECAUSE I **CAN'T**!

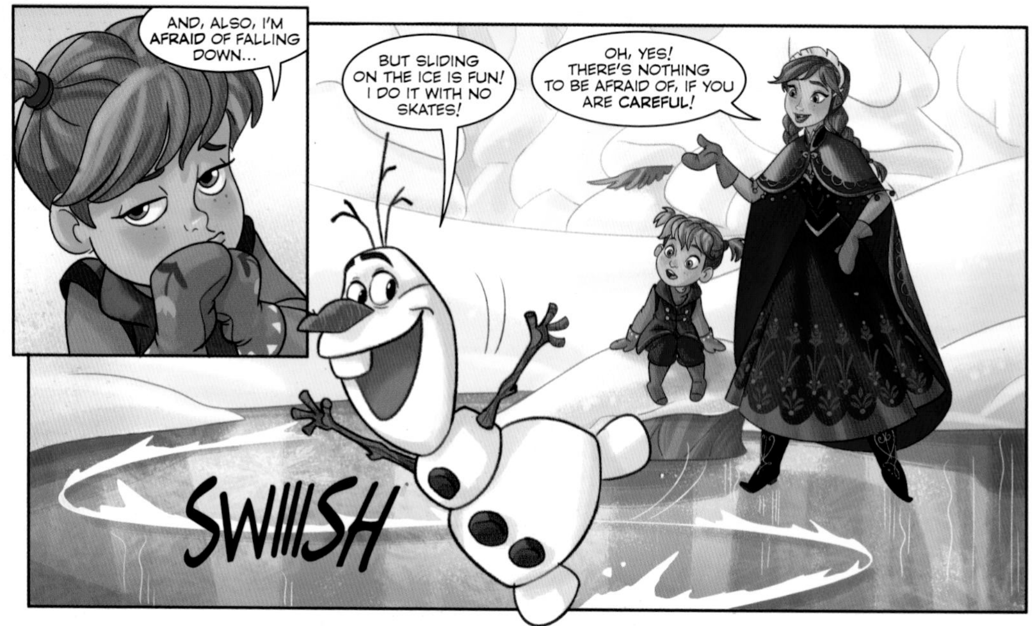
AND, ALSO, I'M **AFRAID** OF FALLING DOWN...
BUT SLIDING ON THE ICE IS FUN! I DO IT WITH NO SKATES!
OH, YES! THERE'S NOTHING TO BE AFRAID OF, IF YOU ARE **CAREFUL**!
SWIIIISH

COME ON AND JOIN YOUR FRIENDS!
I'D LIKE TO, BUT...I CAN'T!
BACK AT THE CASTLE, ANNA AND OLAF TELL ELSA AND KRISTOFF ABOUT MATHILDE...
SHE LOOKED SO GLUM!
TOO BAD SHE'S AFRAID OF ICE. ICE IS WONDERFUL!
MAYBE I CAN GIVE HER ICE SKATING LESSONS HERE AT THE CASTLE!
THAT'S A GREAT IDEA! WITH A TEACHER LIKE YOU, SHE'LL LEARN IN NO TIME!
I'LL NEED YOUR HELP, THOUGH.
WE'LL GO GET HER!
IN THE MEANTIME, I'LL PREPARE THE ICE RINK!
WOOSH
THIS SHOULD BE FUN!

BACK TO THE CASTLE...

HERE IS YOUR ICE SKATING TEACHER, MATHILDE.

QUEEN **ELSA**!

WELCOME, MATHILDE! ARE YOU **READY** TO START?

EVERYONE JOINS IN...
SWISH
SWOOSH
LOOK AT US! THIS IS WHAT YOU **SHOULDN'T** DO!

BEND YOUR KNEES SLIGHTLY AND MOVE ONE FOOT AT A TIME!
OOOOKAY!
THUD

I ALWAYS FALL, BUT I KEEP **PRACTICING**!

SOON, MATHILDE GAINS MORE CONFIDENCE...
I **LOVE** SKATING!
ME TOO!
AND YOU'RE BOTH IMPROVING A LOT!

AFTER SEVERAL LESSONS...
GO MATHILDE GO!
YOU'RE SO GOOD!
SWISH

HOW DID YOU LEARN TO SKATE SO WELL?
QUEEN ELSA TAUGHT ME! AND HER FRIENDS HELPED.

I WANT TO LEARN FROM THEM, TOO!
CAN YOU GIVE US A LESSON?
HUH?!?

IT'LL BE A PLEASURE TO HAVE SO MANY LOVELY STUDENTS!
YAY! MORE LESSONS!
HURRAY!

I THINK I LOVE BEING AN ICE-SKATING TEACHER!
I DON'T KNOW WHY, BUT I WAS SURE ABOUT IT!

The End

SCARY NOISE

Manuscript: Tea Orsi; Layout: Nicoletta Baldari; Cleanup: Miriam Gambino; Color: Stefania Santi

ROOOOAAAAARRR
IT'S BEHIND THIS BUSH! LET'S GO!
I'M READY... I GUESS!
ONE, TWO...
TWO AND A HALF...

...THREE!
ROAAAAAR
KRISTOFF?!?

HUH?! WHAT'S GOING ON? I WAS HAVING SUCH A GREAT NAP!
WE HEARD YOU!
SORRY, WE WOKE YOU.
WHY ARE YOU CARRYING SUCH BIG BOOKS?
OH...WE WANTED TO...SUGGEST YOU READ A GOOD BOOK BEFORE YOUR AFTERNOON NAP!
BUT MAYBE IT'S BETTER IF YOU STAY AWAKE!

The End

TEAM SPIRIT

Manuscript: Tea Orsi; Layout: Alberto Zanon; Cleanup: Letizia Baldari; Color: Angela Capolupo

SOON, IN THE MOUNTAINS...
READY, STEADY... GO!
COME ON, TEAM ARENDELLE!

WHOA!
IT'S LIKE WE ARE A GIANT SNOWBALL!
SWOOOSH

HOLD TIGHT, OLAF!
DON'T WORRY, I...

OOOOH!
OLAF! WATCH OUT!

AHHH!

ARE YOU OKAY, OLAF?
I AM, ARE YOU?

DID YOU HURT YOUR FOOT?
NO... IT'S NOTHING SERIOUS...

ARE YOU SURE? YOU SHOULD REST A BIT!
NO WAY! I'M FINE... REALLY.

AFTER THE ICE-SKATING PRACTICE...
LET ME TAKE A LOOK AT YOUR FOOT.
OUCH! NOW IT HURTS!

IT LOOKS SWOLLEN. I THINK YOU NEED TO STAY OFF OF IT.
YEAH, YOU NEED TO REST FOR A FEW DAYS!
I CAN'T REST! THE GAMES ARE TOMORROW!

YOU'LL STILL BE ON OUR TEAM, ANNA!
YOU'RE RIGHT, OLAF! I MIGHT NOT BE ABLE TO SKATE...

... BUT I CAN HELP PREPARE THE BEST PERFORMANCE EVER!
GREAT! YOU'LL BE OUR COACH!

GET READY FOR THE BIG FINALE!
OOOOKAY!
THREE, TWO, ONE...
SWISH

PERFECT!
CLAP
CLAP

OOOHHH!
THANK YOU!

I'M SO PROUD OF YOU! NOW LET'S PRACTICE THE SLALOM!

SO...
GO! FASTER!
SWISH

WHOAAAAAA!

THANK YOU, COACH ANNA!
WE ARE MORE THAN READY NOW!
OH, I WISH I COULD RACE WITH YOU!

BUT I WILL JUST CHEER AS MUCH AS I CAN!
GOOD IDEA!
UHM...

WHAT ARE YOU THINKING ABOUT, ELSA?
I'LL TELL YOU LATER...

NEXT DAY, BEFORE THE GUESTS ARRIVE...
TA-DA!
EVERYTHING'S READY! DO YOU LIKE IT?
I CAN'T BELIEVE IT!
BESIDES BEING OUR COACH, YOU'LL ALSO BE ON THE TRACK WITH US!
NOW, THAT'S SOME ICE!
BRILLIANT! NOW, LET'S TRY THE TRACK AGAIN! READY, STEADY...
I SEE ANNA GOT COMPLETELY INTO THE COACH'S PART!
YES, MAYBE A BIT TOO MUCH!

The End

Gift Galore

Manuscript: Tea Orsi; Layout: Alberto Zanon; Cleanup: Nicoletta Baldari; Color: Stefania Santi

The End

THE SNOW TROLL

Manuscript: Alessandro Ferrari; Layout: Elisabetta Melaranci;
Cleanup: Federica Salfo; Ink: Michela Frare; Color: Dario Calabria

The End

FLOOD DANGER

Manuscript: Tea Orsi; Layout: Alberto Zanon; Cleanup: Letizia Algeri; Color: MichelAngela World

WOOOSH
NO! IT WASN'T!
I'M AFRAID OUR HIKE IS OVER!
OH NO!
LET'S FIND SOME SHELTER!
QUICK!
LUCKILY...
LOOK! THERE'S A HOUSE OVER THERE!
LET'S GO AND ASK IF WE CAN GO IN!
SO...
KNOCK KNOCK

AND...

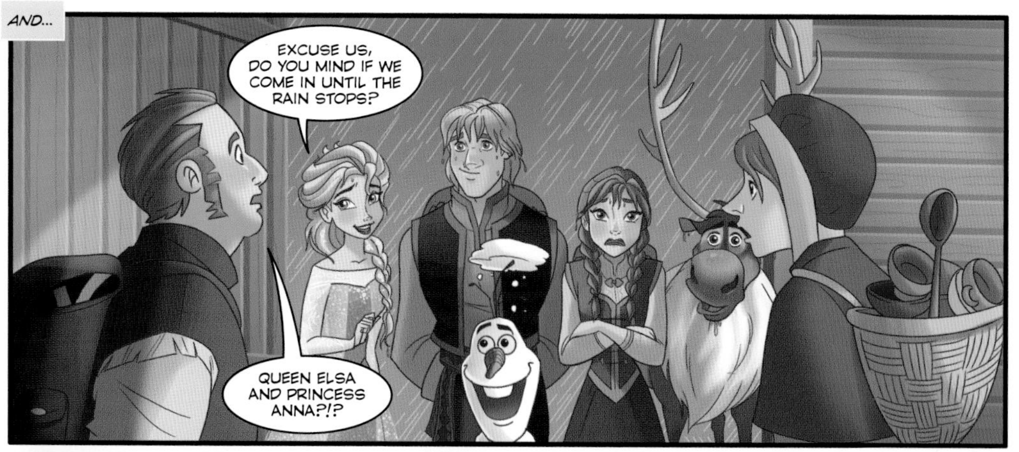
EXCUSE US, DO YOU MIND IF WE COME IN UNTIL THE RAIN STOPS?
QUEEN ELSA AND PRINCESS ANNA?!?

OH, I'VE **NEVER** BEEN HUGGED BY A SNOWMAN!
MY NAME IS OLAF AND I LIKE WARM HUGS!

ARE YOU GETTING READY FOR A **JOURNEY**?
KIND OF, PRINCESS ANNA! I'M AFRAID WE ALL SHOULD **LEAVE** SOON!

LEAVE?!? WHY?
THE RIVER MIGHT **OVERFLOW** ANY MINUTE NOW! STAYING HERE IS **NOT SAFE!**

WE BUILT BARRIERS, BUT IT HAS BEEN RAINING TOO MUCH!
THE WATER LEVEL IS RISING BY THE MINUTE!

STAYING HERE IS TOO DANGEROUS FOR YOU!
WHY DON'T WE TRY TO BUILD HIGHER BARRIERS?

THE RAIN IS TOO HEAVY! WE WON'T BE ABLE TO WORK OUTSIDE!

WHAT CAN WE DO? THE WATER WILL FLOOD OUR HOUSE AND OUR FIELDS!

LET'S CHECK THE WATER LEVEL!
YEAH, THERE'S NO TIME TO WASTE!

THERE MUST BE A WAY TO STOP IT! WHAT ABOUT USING YOUR POWERS?
IT'S WORTH A TRY!

LET'S SEE!
WHHHHHOSSSSSH

AND THE MAGIC WORKS!
THAT'S AMAZING!

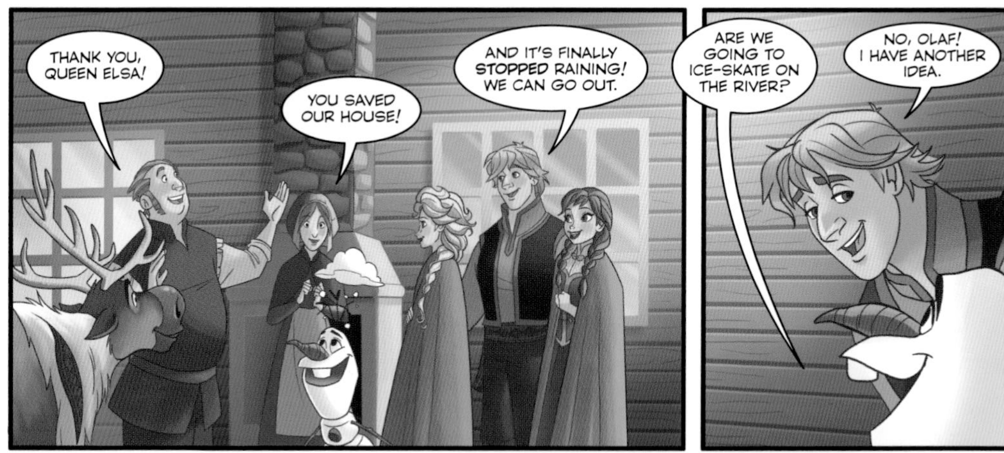
THANK YOU, QUEEN ELSA!
YOU SAVED OUR HOUSE!
AND IT'S FINALLY STOPPED RAINING! WE CAN GO OUT.
ARE WE GOING TO ICE-SKATE ON THE RIVER?
NO, OLAF! I HAVE ANOTHER IDEA.

AND...
WHEN I'M DONE I WILL TAKE THE ICE TO THE MOUNTAINS!
SO IT WON'T BE DANGEROUS WHEN IT MELTS!
PICK
PICK

GOOD JOB, ELSA!
I COULDN'T HAVE DONE IT WITHOUT YOU! WE'RE THE BEST TEAM EVER!

The End

A NEW GAME

Manuscript: Tea Orsi; Layout: Manuela Razzi; Cleanup: Manuela Razzi; Color: Dario Calabria

IT'S GREAT THAT THE SNOWGIES CAN **ENJOY** CURLING AS MUCH AS WE DO!

AND SOMETHING TELLS ME THAT WE'LL GET TO SLIDE MORE STONES THAN EVER!

The End

A Great Song

Manuscript: Tea Orsi; Layout and Cleanup: Elisabetta Melaranci; Color: Dario Calabria

The End

Icy Lights

Manuscript: Tea Orsi ; Layout: Manuela Razzi; Cleanup: Manuela Razzi; Color: Maria Claudia Di Genova

A Wolf at the Door

Manuscript: Alessandro Ferrari; Layout: Federica Salfo; Cleanup: Teresa Geer, Marino Gentile; Ink: Michela Frare; Color: Dario Calabria

OLAF... I REALLY BELIEVE A WOLF IS A PROBLEM.

A HAIRY PROBLEM, WITH FANGS! **SHARP** AND **HORRIBLE** FANGS!
NASTY, **CRUEL** AND **SAVAGE** EYES! REALLY SCARY!
NOT TO MENTION THE EYES!

WELL... MAYBE THIS WOLF IS DIFFERENT. MAYBE THIS WOLF IS **GENTLE** AND **ALONE** AND REALLY **SCARED**...

WOLVES ARE DANGEROUS, OLAF.
THEY'VE TRIED TO EAT HIM ONCE.
TWICE, ACTUALLY.

OKAY, BUT... AREN'T WOLVES **AFRAID TOO**?
...

ALRIGHT... YOU'VE CONVINCED ME, OLAF. WE'LL GO AND **CHECK**.
THANK YOU, ELSA!

WAIT, WHAT? IT'S TOO DANGEROUS!
FSHHH
DON'T WORRY, ANNA. I CAN TAKE CARE OF MYSELF!
I'LL COME WITH YOU! I KNOW HOW TO DEAL WITH WOLVES!
YES, SHE DOES! BUT I'M JOINING YOU THREE. JUST TO BE SURE.
OF COURSE, SVEN IS COMING, TOO.
!
OKAY THEN. WE'LL ALL GO AFTER THE WOLF! TOGETHER WE'LL FIND OUT IF IT'S REALLY DANGEROUS OR NOT...
I BET IT'S NOT.

A LITTLE LATER, IN THE WOODS NEAR ARENDELLE...
WHAT DO WE DO WHEN WE SEE THE WOLF?
WE CAN PET IT, PLAY WITH IT AND, MAYBE, EVEN READ THE WOLF A STORY.

I'M READY!
I MEAN IN CASE HE'S DANGEROUS.

LOOK! THERE IT IS! THERE IT IS!

THAT'S NOT A WOLF, OLAF. IT'S A SQUIRREL!

BUT IT'S SO CUTE IT LOOKED LIKE A WOLF.
YOU'RE KIDDING ME NOW, AREN'T YOU?

LOOK! THERE IT IS!

OHHH, IT'S JUST A SNOW FOX. I LIKE SNOW FOXES BUT I WISH IT WERE...
GRRRR

!
DID YOU HEAR THAT?
THE WOLF...

WAIT, ANNA! IT MIGHT BE DANGEROUS... THIS IS A REAL WOLF!
KRISTOFF? YOU KNOW...

... YOU'RE RIGHT THIS TIME!
GRRRR

NO WAY. IT'S...
... A PUP!
GENTLE AND ALONE AND REALLY SCARED...

I THINK IT MIGHT BE HUNGRY... DO WE HAVE ANYTHING TO EAT?

GOOD IDEA, SVEN! CARROTS ARE PERFECT!

DON'T WORRY, LITTLE ONE... I'M YOUR FRIEND.
SNIFF SNIFF

IT LOOKS LIKE OLAF WAS RIGHT THIS TIME. NOT ALL WOLVES ARE BAD...
SURELY NOT THIS LITTLE ONE HERE!
OHHH! HELLO, WOLFY!

The End

It's Bath Time!

Manuscript: Alessandro Ferrari; Layout: Alberto Zanon; Cleanup: Letizia Algeri; Color: MichelAngela World

COME ON, BUDDY! WHERE ARE YOU?

HEY!

WE CAN PLAY HIDE AND SEEK AFTER A BATH... I PROMISE!

I'M SURE HE'S IN HERE SOMEWHERE.

NOW YOU'RE
JUST BEING
RIDICULOUS!

THIS COULD
GO ON FOREVER!

I HAVE
AN IDEA... I'LL BE
RIGHT BACK!

AN HOUR
LATER...
SNIFF

?
SNIFF

CARROTS
NEVER FAIL
WITH HIM!

!!!

AND NOW, IT'S BATH TIME!
WOOOOSH

A FEW MOMENTS LATER...
WE DID IT!
MMM... YOU SMELL LIKE FRESH CUT PINE NOW, BUDDY.

WELL, AT LEAST WE KNOW HOW TO CATCH HIM NEXT TIME!

The End

Northern Lights Hike

THE NEXT CRYSTAL CEREMONY IS JUST A FEW HOURS AWAY.
WE WOULDN'T MISS IT, KRISTOFF!
REMEMBER LAST TIME, WHEN LITTLE ROCK EARNED HIS TRACKING CRYSTAL? I LOVED SEEING THE NORTHERN LIGHTS!

Manuscript: Georgia Ball; Layout: Benedetta Barone; Cleanup: Michela Cacciatore; Color: Kat Maximenko, Cecilia Giumento, Julia Pinchuk, Alessandra Bracaglia

ONE OF YOUR CRYSTALS ISN'T GLOWING YET--
DON'T YOU NEED ALL OF THEM FOR THE CEREMONY?
YES...IT'S MY CLIMBING CRYSTAL.
"I'VE BEEN TRYING FOR AGES TO MAKE IT GLOW--BUT EVERY TIME I GO OUT TO PROVE I CAN DO IT ON MY OWN--"
RUSTLE RUSTLE
"... SOMEONE ALWAYS HAS HELPFUL ADVICE--"
OH! ARE YOU TRYING TO CLIMB TANGLEROOT CANYON? I DID THAT ONE YESTERDAY.
THE ROOTS AREN'T STRONG ENOUGH FOR SPIKES, SO USE THE ROCKS-- AND WATCH OUT FOR WOODPECKERS!
GOOD HOLDS
"EVEN WHEN I'M ALONE!"

WE ARE ONE BIG, HELPFUL FAMILY.
TOO HELPFUL! I CAN'T SHOW THIS CRYSTAL I **KNOW** HOW TO CLIMB IF EVERYONE KEEPS **TELLING** ME HOW TO CLIMB.
BUT I'VE GOT A PLAN.
I'VE ALWAYS WANTED TO SEE THE ICE CAVE. IT'S A SHORT HIKE UP THAT MOUNTAIN, AND I **KNOW** NONE OF THE OTHER TROLLS HAVE BEEN THERE BEFORE.
BUT THE LAST PART IS NEARLY STRAIGHT UP.
DON'T YOU NEED A PARTNER FOR A CLIMB LIKE THAT?
I GUESS THAT WON'T WORK.
I'D LOVE TO SEE THE ICE CAVE!
WELL... OK.
BUT YOU HAVE TO LET **ME** GET US THERE--NO ADVICE!
WE PROMISE!
I'LL GO TELL GRAND PABBIE WHERE YOU ARE. WE'LL WAIT DOWN HERE FOR YOU.
YEAH, I'M GOING TO TRY TO GROW A MUSHROOM ON MY BACK LIKE THE LITTLE TROLLS DO!
DON'T START THE CEREMONY WITHOUT US!

AFTER LOADING THEIR EQUIPMENT...
IF I CAN GET TO THE ICE CAVES AND BACK IN TIME FOR THE CEREMONY--
THEN MY CLIMBING CRYSTAL WILL GLOW FOR SURE!

ACCORDING TO MY MAP, AND THAT TREE STUMP THAT LOOKS LIKE A SQUIRREL, THIS IS THE WAY.
REMEMBER, NO ADVICE!

NOTHING FROM ME!

I CAN SEE THE CAVE!
IT'S JUST A SHORT CLIMB FROM HERE.

WHACK
WHACK
WHACK
WE'RE ALMOST THERE.
WAIT UNTIL ELSA HEARS ABOUT THIS!

IT'S GETTING LATE-- WE NEED TO SPEED THINGS UP.

MAYBE I COULD USE THE PITON THAT'S ALREADY THERE? IT LOOKS KIND OF OLD.
IT'S PROBABLY OKAY.

THE PITON HELD OUR WEIGHT WITHOUT ANY TROUBLE.
I'M GLAD I SAVED US SOME TIME!

CREAK

CHUNK

GASP

KRISTOFF!
ARE YOU ALL RIGHT?!
I'M NOT HURT...
BUT I LOST MY ICE AX. I DON'T THINK I CAN GET FAR WITHOUT HELP.

OPAL?
WHAT DO I DO? WHAT DO I DO? THINK...

I... I DON'T KNOW HOW TO GET HIM OUT, ANNA.
I NEED ADVICE.

DON'T FEEL BAD, OPAL. EVERYONE NEEDS TO ASK FOR HELP SOMETIMES.
I'LL TALK YOU THROUGH IT. UNTIE THE ROPE FROM THE ROCK, THEN START BACK DOWN.

I'M SO HAPPY YOU'RE ALL RIGHT!
IT WAS MY FAULT, KRISTOFF. I MADE A MISTAKE.

I'VE MADE PLENTY OF MISTAKES. JUST ASK SVEN.
SHOULD WE TRY AGAIN?
NO, WE'LL MISS THE CEREMONY.

I'M PROUD OF YOU, OPAL. LOOK HOW CLOSE WE GOT TO THE ICE CAVES!

I'LL GET THERE NEXT TIME!

I'M JUST SORRY I COULDN'T LEAD YOU BOTH TO THE CAVE SAFELY.
I GUESS I'LL JUST HAVE TO WAIT FOR THE NEXT CRYSTAL CEREMONY.

GASP

WHY IS MY CLIMBING CRYSTAL GLOWING, GRAND PABBIE?
WE DIDN'T REACH THE ICE CAVE. MY FRIEND COULD HAVE BEEN HURT AND IT WAS ALL MY FAULT!

MISTAKES ARE HOW WE LEARN, OPAL.
THE CRYSTAL KNOWS YOU LEARNED AN IMPORTANT LESSON ABOUT SAFETY TODAY THAT YOU'LL ALWAYS REMEMBER.

IT'S CLEAR YOU CAN BE SUCCESSFUL IN ANYTHING YOU SET YOUR MIND TO--
AS LONG AS YOU HAVE FRIENDS.

The End

An Original Decor

Manuscript: Tea Orsi; Layout: Alberto Zanon; Cleanup: Miriam Gambino; Color: Stefania Santi

YOU'RE RIGHT, OLAF! AND IN FACT...

...I JUST NEED SOME RIBBONS AND... YOUR HELP!
WHAT DO YOU HAVE IN MIND, ELSA?

AND, AFTER A LOT OF WORK...
I'VE NEVER SEEN SUCH ORIGINAL DECORATIONS! THANK YOU!
THIS LOOKS SO FESTIVE!

AND IT WILL ALSO GIVE THE CUSTOMERS GREAT IDEAS FOR WINTER GIFTS!
HAPPY HOLIDAYS!

The End

Easier Said than Done

Manuscript: Tea Orsi; Layout: Nicoletta Baldari; Cleanup: Nicoletta Baldari; Color: Dario Calabria

The End

Amazing Nose

Manuscript: Tea Orsi; Layout: Emilio Urbano; Cleanup: Marino Gentile; Ink: Michela Frare; Color: Antonella Angrisani

The End

THE POLAR BEAR PIPER

Part 1

Original Story by Erica David; Adapted by Chantal Pericoli; Layout: Manuela Razzi; Clean: Benedetta Barone; Color: MichelAngela World

OH, PRINCESS ANNA! THANK YOU FOR COMING. IT'S MY PIES! THEY ARE, WELL... SEE FOR YOURSELF.

I LEFT THEM TO COOL. BUT NOW THEY ARE GONE.
HMM... CHERRY?

...CHERRY!
OOH, CHERRY!

IT'S NOT JUST MY SHOP THAT'S BEEN SWINDLED, YOU KNOW. YOU SHOULD ALSO SPEAK WITH ELIN AT THE **WHARF**.

AND SO...
IT'S BEEN UNUSUALLY WARM LATELY, AND WE'VE CAUGHT MORE FISH THAN EVER! BUT SOME OF OUR FISH HAVE GONE MISSING.

BY THE WAY, YOU MIGHT WANT TO SPEAK WITH LEANDER AT THE LAUNDRY. I HEARD SOMETHING ODD HAS GONE ON OVER THERE, TOO.

HAVE YOU HEARD ABOUT ALL THIS MYSTERIOUS **MISCHIEF**?
THE ICE HARVESTERS ARE SAYING THIS COULD BE THE WORK OF **POLAR BEARS**!

POLAR BEARS? I DON'T THINK SO. THEY LIVE IN THE ARCTIC. THAT'S MUCH FARTHER NORTH.

LATER, AT THE LAUNDRY...
AT LEAST LEANDER DIDN'T LOSE HER CHEERFUL MOOD. DESPITE THE MESS, SHE'S HUMMING HER **USUAL TUNE**!

OOOPS...

GUYS! I CAN'T SEE! IT'S AN ETERNAL NIGHT!

DAYLIGHT!

THOSE LOOK LIKE BEAR TRACKS TO ME.
THERE'S ONLY ONE THING LEFT TO DO: FOLLOW THESE TRACKS!

AND SO, DEEP IN THE FOREST...
OH, I'VE ALWAYS WANTED TO SEE A POLAR BEAR! THEY ARE FLUFFY AND SWEET!
OLAF, POLAR BEARS ARE **FEROCIOUS** AND **HUGE**.

THIS LOOKS LIKE THE REMAINS OF ONE OF TILDA'S PIES!

WHAT HAVE YOU GOT THERE, BUDDY?

LOOKS LIKE MORE FISH BONES AND... A SWEATER?
IT MIGHT HAVE COME FROM THE LAUNDRY.

THESE BONES HAVE QUITE AN ODOR...
I KNOW, BUT IT'S IMPORTANT TO COLLECT ALL THE EVIDENCE, WHEN YOU'RE WORKING ON A CASE!

WHAT WOULD WE DO IF WE ACTUALLY FIND A POLAR BEAR?

WE SHOULD HIDE!
WE SHOULD MAKE FRIENDS WITH THE BEARS. I BET THEY GIVE EXCELLENT HUGS!

CRICK
CRACK

SEE? LOOK HOW CUTE THEY ARE! I TOLD YOU THAT POLAR BEARS WOULD MAKE GREAT FRIENDS!

GROOOWL
OR MAYBE NOT...
UH-OH... THAT MUST BE THE MAMA!

GROOOWWL

SWISH

I GUESS POLAR BEARS ARE PRETTY USED TO CRASHING THROUGH ICE AND SNOW, HUH?
CRACK

WHAT ARE YOU DOING?
JUST WAIT!

ANNA, THAT WAS **GENIUS**! THE BEAR IS DISTRACTED BY THE SMELL OF THE FISH BONES INSIDE THE BAG!
SNIFF
SNIFF

NOW LET'S GET BACK TO THE CASTLE! WE'LL COME BACK WHEN WE'RE MORE PREPARED...

End of Part 1

THE POLAR BEAR PIPER

Original Story by Erica David; Adapted by Chantal Pericoli; Layout: Manuela Razzi; Clean: Benedetta Barone; Color: MichelAngela World

A FEW HOURS LATER, MANY VILLAGERS COME TO HELP CLEAN THE GARBAGE PILE...
YOUR IDEA TO RECRUIT HELP WAS GREAT!

I THINK THERE'S A WAY WE COULD SALVAGE SOME OF THIS STUFF...

ELSA? THE FARMERS COULD USE A LOT OF THIS STUFF AS **COMPOST**!

GREAT IDEA, ANNA! AND I BET WE CAN FIND A USE FOR ALL THIS BROKEN GLASS AND THESE OLD BOTTLES, TOO!

LATER THAT AFTERNOON...
TO THANK YOU ALL, I'LL INVITE EVERYONE TO A PARTY AT THE CASTLE TOMORROW NIGHT!

THE FOLLOWING NIGHT...

AND SO...
IF THE POLAR BEARS TRAVELLED FROM THE ARCTIC ON AN ICE FLOE, THEN TRAVELLING ON AN ICE FLOE IS THE WAY FOR THEM TO GET BACK.

BUT THIS UNUSUALLY WARM WEATHER MUST HAVE MELTED THEIR ICE FLOE, STRANDING THEM HERE ON THE MAINLAND.

THERE ISN'T ANY MORE ICE IN THE HARBOR. SO THERE'S NO CHANCE THAT OUR BEARS CAN CLIMB ONTO AN **ICEBERG** AND DRIFT HOME, UNLESS...

...UNLESS I USE MY MAGIC TO MAKE ONE.

NOW, WE COULD LURE THEM TO THE ICEBERG WITH FOOD, OR...
MUSIC!

THE DAY AFTER...
THIS IS SO EXCITING! I'M GOING TO BE A REAL PIED PIPER.
I HOPE THESE POLAR BEARS REALLY LIKE MUSIC!

IT'S SO OBVIOUS: WHAT COULD HAVE ATTRACTED THE BEARS TO THE VILLAGE? LEANDER ALWAYS HUMS! OLAF, YOU CAN DO THIS...

AND SO...

NICE WORK, OLAF!

AND NOW AN ICY WIND TO CARRY OUR FRIENDS RIGHT BACK TO THEIR ARCTIC HOME...

THREE CHEERS FOR THE POLAR BEAR PIPER!

QUEEN ELSA, PRINCESS ANNA, THE PEOPLE OF ARENDELLE WOULD LIKE TO PRESENT YOU WITH THESE GIFTS.

THIS VASE HAS BEEN MADE ENTIRELY FROM **GLASS SHARDS** RECYCLED FROM THE TRASH PILE.

AND ALSO, THANK YOU FOR THE COMPOST!
!

AHAHAH!
STUCK

The End

Yummy Snowflakers

Manuscript: Tea Orsi; Layout: Emilio Urbano;
Cleanup: Veronica Di Lorenzo; Color: Dario Calabria

SOON...

AND FINALLY...
GOOD! WE CAN START MAKING THE **FROSTING** NOW!
FROSTING?!? BUT I'M **STARVING**!

DON'T WORRY, ANNA!

THIS WON'T TAKE LONG!
WHOA!
AND JUST A SPRINKLE OF SUGAR!
THESE TRULY ARE **SNOWFLAKE** COOKIES!
AND THEY ARE NICE INDEED!

The End

A Surprise for Everyone

THE BARON OF AKERSELVA AND HIS FAMILY ARE IN ARENDELLE FOR AN IMPORTANT NEGOTIATION.

YOU CAN START BUILDING THE NEW BRIDGE SOON, BARON!

THANK YOU FOR BEING SO UNDERSTANDING, YOUR MAJESTIES!

IT'LL BE EXTREMELY USEFUL, EVEN FOR ARENDELLE'S FARMERS.

CAN I SEE THE CASTLE NOW, MOMMY? I'M SO BORED!

POCK

CASPAR!!!

OH, DON'T WORRY, BARONESS!

I'D LOVE TO GIVE CASPAR A LITTLE TOUR!

Manuscript: Tea Orsi; Layout and Cleanup: Sara Storino; Color: Dario Calabria

THIS IS THE ART ROOM! DO YOU LIKE PAINTING?
I LOVE PAINTING! IT'S MY SPECIALTY.

HEY! WHAT'S THAT?

IT'S A **SURPRISE** FOR YOUR FATHER!
CAN I SEE IT?

IF YOU WAIT UNTIL AFTER DINNER, IT'LL BE A SURPRISE FOR YOU, TOO.
EXCUSE ME, PRINCESS, QUEEN ELSA WOULD LIKE YOU TO BE PRESENT DURING THE NEGOTIATIONS.

I'LL BE BACK SOON. WHY DON'T YOU PAINT SOMETHING IN THE MEANTIME?
HMM...

LATER...
THIS HAS BEEN A WONDEFUL VISIT TO ARENDELLE, QUEEN ELSA.
I'M HAPPY YOU ENJOYED IT!

TO THANK YOU FOR YOUR VISIT, WE HAVE SOMETHING FOR YOU.

A GIFT FOR YOU FROM ARENDELLE.
OH, WHAT A WONDERFUL SURPRISE!

SWOOSH
GASP!
SURPRISE!

I-I-I'M SO SORRY, I...
DO YOU LIKE THE MOUSTACHE, DADDY? I PAINTED IT MYSELF!

MOM ALWAYS SAYS A MOUSTACHE WOULD SUIT YOU, BUT YOU NEVER LISTEN TO HER!
WELL, NOW THAT I SEE THIS...

I ADMIT SHE MIGHT BE RIGHT! PERHAPS I WILL GROW ONE AFTER ALL.

THANK YOU! WITHOUT THIS PORTRAIT I WOULD HAVE NEVER CONVINCED HIM!
OH, IT SEEMS YOU HAVE YOUR SON TO THANK AS WELL!
YES, CASPAR MADE IT A MASTERPIECE!

The End

DANCING DAY

Manuscript: Alessandro Ferrari; Layout: Elisabetta Melaranci; Cleanup: Federica Salfo; Color: Dario Calabria, Stefania Santi

ANNA! WHAT A SURPRISE!

WHAT'S GOING ON?
WHY? WHAT DO YOU MEAN? NOTHING IS GOING... ON.

COME ON! THESE SCULPTURES ARE EVERYWHERE IN THE CASTLE!

WELL... NEXT WEEK THE PRINCES OF FIVE KINGDOMS WILL COME TO ARENDELLE AND I'LL HAVE TO DANCE WITH THEM... BUT I DON'T KNOW HOW TO DANCE AS WELL AS I'D LIKE, SO...

... I MADE THESE STATUES SO I COULD SEE THE MOVES AND LEARN THEM!
!

DON'T YOU WORRY, ELSA... I'LL TEACH YOU HOW TO DANCE!

SO...
ARE YOU SURE?
ABSOLUTELY YES. WHAT COULD POSSIBLY GO WRONG?
LIKE... EVERYTHING?
OW!
FSHOOM
WOW! IT'S SNOWING!
I'M SORRY...

IT'S NOT EASY...

"... BUT IF YOU KEEP PRACTICING..."
SOMEONE STOOOOP ME!

"... AND PRACTICING..."

"... YOU'LL FINALLY MASTER IT!"
YES! I CAN DANCE!
I CAN DANCE TOO! I'M A DANCING SNOWMAN!
GREAT! NOW YOU'RE READY...

"... FOR YOUR OFFICIAL DANCING DAY!"
YOUR MAJESTY...
YOUR HIGHNESS...
BUT AS SOON AS THEY START...
OW!
I'M TERRIBLY SORRY, YOUR MAJESTY. I MUST CONFESS... I AM NOT SUCH A GREAT DANCER AS YOU ARE!
ACTUALLY, QUEEN ELSA...
... NEITHER AM I!
I NEVER LEARNED EITHER!
WE ARE SO ASHAMED...
!
!
WELL... WHAT ABOUT SKATING, INSTEAD?
?

READY? LET'S GO!

FSHOOM

YOUR HIGHNESS?

DON'T WORRY, I AM NOT THAT GOOD EITHER... WE'LL HELP EACH OTHER!

YOU'RE REALLY GOOD!

THANK YOU, YOUR MAJESTY! I LOVE SKATING!

The End

A Fuzzy Rest

Manuscript: Tea Orsi; Layout: Emilio Urbano; Cleanup: Manuela Razzi; Color: Dario Calabria

ERM...MAYBE TODAY'S NOT THE DAY FOR RELAXING!

The End

Perfect Anniversary

Manuscript: Tea Orsi; Layout: Emilio Urbano; Cleanup: Marino Gentile; Color: MichelAngela World

The End

Morning Lesson

Manuscript: Alessandro Ferrari; Layout: Elisabetta Melaranci; Cleanup: Arianna Rea, Federica Salfo; Ink: Michela Frare, Cristina Stella; Color: Dario Calabria

IT'S NOT THAT HARD... I AM DOING GREAT! LET'S DO IT AGAIN AS SOON AS THIS CLIMB IS FINISHED!
DON'T USE THE ROPE, LOOK FOR HANDHOLDS!

BE CAREFUL!
DON'T WORRY, ELSA, KRISTOFF IS AN EXPERT! I AM HAVING A LOT OF FUN!

COME ON, ANNA... YOU MADE IT!

WHOA!

SEE? ISN'T IT BEAUTIFUL?
IT'S... MAGNIFICENT! REALLY WORTH IT!

IF I DIDN'T KNOW ANY BETTER, I WOULD CALL IT A PROPER DATE, KRISTOFF...
IT ISN'T! WELL... I MEAN... IT COULD BE...

The End

Just When You Weren't Looking

Manuscript: Georgia Ball; Layout: Benedetta Barone; Cleanup: Michela Cacciatore; Color: Kat Maximenko, Vita Efremova, Yanna Chinstova, Anastasiia Belousova

GOT A HEADACHE?
TWO HEADACHES, AND THEY BOTH OWN A WAFFLE CART.
OOH! I KNOW WHAT TO DO.
"WHEN YOU'RE ANGRY NOW AND THEN, HOLD YOUR BREATH AND COUNT TO TEN."
I'M NOT SURE HOW THAT WOULD--
GASP
MMON... MMOO... MFEE...
I NEED A NEW APPROACH FOR DEALING WITH BJARNE AND BJORN.
"THEIR CONSTANT ARGUING IS EXHAUSTING."
"I DON'T KNOW HOW TWO BROTHERS CAN GO THAT FAR..."
I WISH I HAD YOUR UNSHAKABLE CHEER, ANNA. HOW DO YOU MANAGE TO STAY SO UPBEAT?
WELL, EVER SINCE I WAS A KID, I DIDN'T BOTHER DWELLING ON WHAT COULD GO WRONG BECAUSE THINGS JUST SEEMED TO WORK OUT EVENTUALLY.

"THIS WHOLE THING REMINDS ME OF HOW MUCH I LOVE WAFFLES. I ALWAYS LOOKED FORWARD TO THE SPECIAL DAYS WHEN OLINA WOULD COOK THEM. BUT ONE TIME I OVERSLEPT..."

"I WAS SO DISAPPOINTED I HAD TO WAIT UNTIL THE NEXT WAFFLE DAY--BUT THEN I FOUND A HOT WAFFLE WAITING FOR ME IN MY ROOM!"
WAFFLE
"OLINA CAN BE SO THOUGHTFUL LIKE THAT, I'M SURE IT WAS HER."

"AND REMEMBER THAT TIME I WRECKED MY BIKE ON THAT VASE IN THE HALL?"
"OH, I GUESS YOU DON'T. ANYWAY, THE NEXT DAY I NOTICED SOMEONE HAD MOVED ALL OF THE FURNITURE FOR ME."
"I NEVER FOUND OUT WHO..."

"OH! AND THERE USED TO BE THIS PICTURE OF ADMIRAL NELSON IN THE SITTING ROOM..."
"I LOVED THAT PAINTING. MOTHER GAVE IT TO THE MARQUIS OF FREDERBORG SO HE'D IMPORT MORE HERRING."
"I WAS DEVASTATED."

"UNTIL THE NEW PAINTING SHOWED UP THAT WAS EVEN BETTER! NO OFFENSE, ADMIRAL."
"NOT SURE WHO WAS BEHIND THAT ONE EITHER--BUT I HAVE MY SUSPICIONS."

I HAVE A CONFESSION TO MAKE.
"I HEARD YOU SNORING ONCE ON WAFFLE DAY AND KNEW YOU'D MISS OUT..."
"MY WAFFLE WAS ALWAYS BROUGHT UP FOR ME SO I ASKED FOR AN EXTRA ONE AND SNEAKED IT INTO YOUR ROOM."
"I DO REMEMBER WHEN YOU CRASHED YOUR BIKE. I HEARD YOU CRYING OUTSIDE MY DOOR."
"I GOT OUT OF BED WHEN EVERYONE ELSE WAS ASLEEP AND MOVED THE FURNITURE OUT OF THE WAY FOR YOU."
"MOTHER DIDN'T KNOW YOU WERE SO FOND OF ADMIRAL NELSON. THEY DID COMMISSION A NEW PAINTING, BUT I ASKED TO ADD MORE SNOW AND I MADE ANOTHER LITTLE SUGGESTION..."

HEY, THAT'S US! I NEVER NOTICED BEFORE.

YOU WERE BRIGHTENING MY DAYS ALL ALONG...EVEN WHEN I DIDN'T KNOW IT.

WE LOST SO MANY YEARS.
HOW COULD YOU FORGET THE LOVE YOU FEEL FOR YOUR BROTHER?
I BET THEY CARE MORE THAN THEY THINK THEY DO AND I KNOW HOW TO PROVE IT.
TELL THEM TO MEET US IN ARENDELLE SQUARE TOMORROW AND LEAVE THE REST TO ME.

I FOUND AN OWL IN MY OVEN THIS MORNING! I DON'T KNOW HOW HE STUFFED THAT THING IN THERE BUT--
AND WHAT ABOUT THE CAT I FOUND IN THE FLOUR?
LOOK! ANNA'S HERE!
BJARNE, BJORN...
I ASKED AROUND ARENDELLE AND SOME OF YOUR NEIGHBORS HAVE A FEW THINGS TO SAY.

YOU PAID ME TO KNIT FOR YOUR BROTHER'S DOG AND ASKED ME NOT TO TELL HIM.
WELL, I'M NOT GOING TO LET THE POOR THING SHIVER.
I WONDERED WHERE HE GOT THAT SWEATER!
I SAW YOU LEAVE A CASSEROLE FOR YOUR BROTHER ONLY TWO DAYS AGO!
THOSE CASSEROLES ARE COMING FROM YOU?
YOU NEVER HAVE TIME TO COOK FOR YOURSELF.
I SECRETLY BUY FROM BOTH OF YOU AND COMBINE MY WAFFLES. HAVE YOU EVER TRIED BERRIES AND CREAM TOGETHER?
SAY... MAYBE WE'VE GOT SOMETHING HERE.
PERHAPS WE SHOULD HAVE BEEN PARTNERS ALL ALONG.
I'LL MANAGE THE MONEY AND YOU CAN DO THE COOKING!
I'VE SEEN YOU DO MATH. I'LL MANAGE THE MONEY!
MAYBE THEY SHOULD NAME THEIR STAND "THE BICKERING BROS."
SO, WHAT'S FOR DINNER?
ANYTHING BUT WAFFLES!

The End

NEW BRANCHES

Manuscript: Tea Orsi; Layout: Emilio Urbano; Cleanup: Rosa La Barbera; Color: Dario Calabria

The End

SNOWGIES ABOARD

IT'S A SPECIAL DAY AT THE ICE PALACE...
FRIDGE, SLUDGE, FLURRY...YEAH! YOU ARE ALL HERE!
BE PATIENT! YOUR TURN WILL COME SOON!
NEXT, PLEASE!
OH, MY LITTLE BROTHERS JUST LOVE SAILING!
GREAT, BUT...

Manuscript: Tea Orsi; Layout: Nicoletta Baldari; Cleanup: Sara Storino; Color: Patrizia Zangrilli

Open Your Eyes

Manuscript: Alessandro Ferrari; Layout: Arianna Rea; Cleanup: Federica Salfo; Ink: Michela Frare, Cristina Stella; Color: Dario Calabria

A SECOND LATER...
OPEN YOUR EYES, SISTER...
I CAN'T BELIEVE I'M DOING THIS!

!
... AND LET YOUR VOICE GO!

AHHHHHH!
AHHHHHH!

THUMPF

YES! YES! YES! LET'S DO IT AGAIN!
I KNEW IT...

The End

A Great Spring Game

Manuscript: Tea Orsi; Layout: Emilio Urbano; Cleanup: Miriam Gambino; Color: Dario Calabria

IT'S A GAME! YOU'LL PLAY IN TEAMS AND WILL HAVE TO FIND SOME ITEMS IN A LIST!
NICE! CAN YOU MAKE A LIST FOR US?

OKAY! YOU AND SVEN CAN CHALLENGE ELSA AND OLAF. WHAT DO YOU THINK?
IT'S GONNA BE EXCITING!

BACK AT THE CASTLE, ANNA TELLS ELSA ABOUT THE HUNT, AND...
I WROTE A LIST FOR EACH TEAM. THE FIRST TO COMPLETE THEIR SEARCH WILL WIN THE GAME!
SOUNDS FUN!

ARE YOU READY FOR THE BIG CHALLENGE?
MORE THAN READY!

LET'S START!
GOOD LUCK, ELSA!

THE HUNT BEGINS!

LATER, IN THE VALLEY...
GREAT! WE'VE GOT THE FIRST ITEM
ANNA?!?

ELSA! DO YOU HAVE TO FIND A LEAF TOO?
NO, I HAVE A CRYSTAL IN MY LIST!

LIKE THOSE?
YES! BUT HOW CAN WE REACH THEM?

WELL, WE ACTUALLY ARE ON RIVAL TEAMS, BUT...

...WE CAN GIVE YOU A LITTLE HELP!
THANK YOU!

A BIT OF TEAM WORK, AND...

BUT THE SISTERS MEET ON NORTH MOUNTAIN TOO, AND...

AND FINALLY...

WE MET IN **ALL** THE THREE PLACES!

YEAH, AND IT SEEMS THAT BOTH OUR TEAMS HAVE JUST **WON** THE GAME!

GREAT! THIS IS **EXACTLY** WHAT I PLANNED!

I LISTED ALL THE PLACES YOU SHOULD GO, BECAUSE I WANTED YOU TO MEET AND ENJOY THE HUNT **TOGETHER**!

NOW I KNOW WHY THE ITEMS WERE SO EASY TO FIND! YOU'RE A **GENIUS**!

AND WE ARE DEFINITELY THE BEST TEAM EVER!

The End

Two is Better Than One

Manuscript: Tea Orsi; Layout: Elisabetta Melaranci; Cleanup: Rosa La Barbera; Color: Dario Calabria

Snow Champion

The End

Manuscript: Alessandro Ferrari; Layout: Nicoletta Baldari; Cleanup: Rosa La Barbera; Color: Stefania Santi

THE LITTLE HOUSE

Manuscript: Tea Orsi; Layout: Alberto Zanon; Cleanup: Nicoletta Baldari; Color: Manuela Nerolini and Ekaterina Makimenko

AFTER A SHORT WALK...

ARE YOU READY TO START?

YEEES!

MORE THAN READY!

HMMM...

VROOOM

OH, NO!

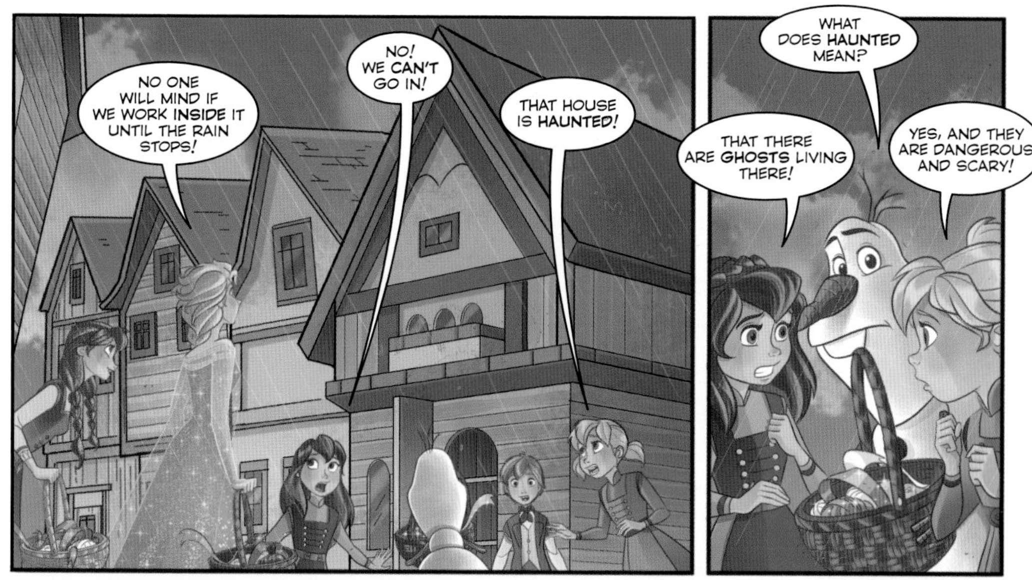
NO ONE WILL MIND IF WE WORK INSIDE IT UNTIL THE RAIN STOPS!
NO! WE CAN'T GO IN!
THAT HOUSE IS HAUNTED!
WHAT DOES HAUNTED MEAN?
THAT THERE ARE GHOSTS LIVING THERE!
YES, AND THEY ARE DANGEROUS AND SCARY!

"SOMETIMES YOU CAN HEAR CREEPY SOUNDS COMING FROM IT, ESPECIALLY WHEN IT'S WINDY!"
SCREEEECH

DON'T BE AFRAID! I'M SURE THERE ARE NO GHOSTS INSIDE THAT HOUSE!
AND IF THERE ARE, WE WILL PROTECT YOU FROM THEM!

ANNA! GHOSTS DON'T EXIST!
WELL, YOU NEVER KNOW...
I'M NOT SCARED! MAYBE THE GHOSTS ARE FRIENDLY!

LET'S GO! THE RAIN IS GETTING HEAVIER!
WHAT SHALL WE DO?
MAYBE WE SHOULD TRY...

BE CAREFUL!
SHRIEK
DON'T WORRY!

WOW! IT'S NOT BAD AT ALL!
THESE GHOSTS HAVE A COZY HOUSE!
SHRIEEEEK
WHAT WAS THAT?!
AHHH! THE GHOSTS ARE COMING!

SHRIEK
NO! IT WAS JUST THE WIND THAT MADE THIS **WINDOW** MOVE, SEE?!
OOOH! THAT'S **TRUE**!
I THINK QUEEN ELSA WAS RIGHT!
MAYBE THE GHOSTS DON'T LIVE HERE **ANYMORE**!
YES! WE CAN STAY HERE AND FINALLY MAKE OUR DECORATIONS!
MAYBE WE SHOULD **CLEAN** UP A LITTLE FIRST!
OUTSIDE, THE RAIN KEEPS FALLING, BUT OUR FRIENDS GET TO WORK...
I DIDN'T THINK THAT CLEANING COULD BE FUN!
EVERYTHING IS FUN WHEN WE DO IT **TOGETHER**!
THE WINDOW WILL STOP MAKING THAT NOISE...
...AND THIS LITTLE HOUSE WILL BE JUST **PERFECT** FOR US!

AND, ON THE NEXT DAY...

DO YOU LIKE OUR HIDEOUT, MOMMY?

IT'S NICE FOR THEM TO HAVE A SAFE PLACE WHERE THEY CAN PLAY TOGETHER!

YOU MADE THE KIDS REALLY HAPPY, ELSA!

AND WE'RE GOING TO VISIT THEM EVEN MORE OFTEN FROM NOW ON!

I WAS JUST ABOUT TO SAY THE SAME THING, OLAF!

The End

MORE ICE, PLEASE!

Manuscript: Tea Orsi; Layout: Alberto Zanon; Cleanup: Manuela Razzi; Color: Dario Calabria

The End

SWIM DREAM

Manuscript: Alessandro Ferrari; Layout: Elisabetta Melaranci; Cleanup: Arianna Rea, Federica Salfo; Ink: Michela Frare, Cristina Stella; Color: Dario Calabria

The End

Restless Week

Writer: Georgia Ball; Layouts: Benedetta Barone; Inks: Michela Cacciatore;
Colors: Ekaterina Maximenko, Yana Chinstova, Anastasiia Beloushova; Letters: AndWorld Design

DO YOU REMEMBER WHAT I HAVE SCHEDULED TODAY, KAI?
YES, QUEEN ELSA. THERE'S A LOT TO DO BEFORE THE DELEGATES FROM BORDIGNON ARRIVE.

YOU HAVE A MEETING WITH THE HEAD OF THE FISHERMAN'S GUILD...AND THE BOOK YOU ORDERED ON BORDIGNESE CUSTOMS ARRIVED...
I KNOW HOW MUCH ARENDELLE WOULD BENEFIT FROM TRADE WITH BORDIGNON. WE SHOULD DO EVERYTHING WE CAN TO MAKE SURE THAT DINNER IS PERFECT.
I HAVE A SPEECH TO WRITE, BUT FIRST--

"--I HAVE A VERY IMPORTANT APPOINTMENT."
QUEEN ELSA!!!

I'M SO PLEASED YOU VOLUNTEERED TO HELP WITH THE READING CONTEST THIS YEAR, QUEEN ELSA...
...THE CHILDREN GET A LITTLE STRAW SNOWFLAKE FOR EVERY BOOK THEY'VE READ THIS MONTH.
AND YOUR IDEA IS SO INVENTIVE--DECORATING THE CLASSROOM LIKE A WINTER WONDERLAND WILL MAKE THE DAY I GIVE OUT PRIZES EXTRA SPECIAL!

I JUST KNOW THE ROOM WILL BE QUITE LOVELY--
--BUT YOUR ROYAL DUTIES MUST KEEP YOU SO BUSY, ARE YOU SURE I'M NOT IMPOSING?
YAWN OF COURSE YOU'RE NOT IMPOSING...

...I WANT TO HELP--AND ENCOURAGE YOUNG READERS!

WE'LL NEED A SNOWFLAKE WREATH FOR EVERY BOOK THE CHILDREN READ, I WONDER HOW MANY THAT WILL BE?
YAWN I SHOULD READ AT LEAST **ONE** CHAPTER OF MY BOOK ON BORDIGNON CUSTOMS.
MAYBE I'LL JUST REST MY EYES FOR A SECOND...

ELSA, WAKE UP!
I THINK YOU WERE HAVING A NIGHTMARE...

...IS EVERYTHING OKAY?
I THINK SO, ANNA. IT'S JUST-- I KEEP DREAMING I'M BEING PULLED THIS WAY AND THAT...
I'M SORRY TO INTERRUPT, BUT IT'S TIME FOR YOUR MEETING...

...THE BORDIGNESE ARE INTERESTED IN TRADING THEIR FABRIC PRINTS FOR MORE COD. WE NEED TO DISCUSS THE TERMS...
...I JUST HOPE I STAY AWAKE LONG ENOUGH TO FINISH MY SPEECH...
YAWN

Each night Elsa wakes up from another anxious dream...
I THINK I'LL DONATE A FEW BOOKS TO THE SCHOOL FOR THE CONTEST... *YAWN*

ARE YOU *SURE* YOU'RE NOT SLEEPY?
BECAUSE YOUR MOUTH KEEPS OPENING REALLY WIDE...
YAWN I'M A LITTLE TIRED, OLAF, BUT THERE'S NO TIME TO REST...
...I HAVE TO GET THESE BOOKS TO THE SCHOOL BEFORE THE READING CONTEST ENDS...

HI FRIENDS!
I WISH THERE WERE THREE OF *ME.* THEN IF THREE PEOPLE INVITED ME TO SOMETHING FUN I WOULDN'T HAVE TO PICK JUST ONE...
...IF THERE WERE THREE OF ME, I COULD GET EVERYTHING DONE...

...MAYBE *THAT'S* WHY I'M HAVING ANXIOUS DREAMS...
...I'M TRYING TO DO TOO MANY THINGS AT ONCE!
I'M ONLY ONE PERSON, BUT I KNOW WHERE I CAN FIND TWO MORE...
...AND A SNOWMAN!

I HAD NO IDEA YOU WERE SO OVERWHELMED!
I'LL READ EVERY BOOK ON BORDIGNON I CAN FIND AND HELP YOU PREPARE.
I'LL MAKE WALL DECORATIONS OUT OF CLOTH AND WEAVE THE STRAW WREATHS...
OOH! CAN I HELP?
AND THAT WILL GIVE *ME* TIME TO WRITE MY SPEECH.

The big day arrives...
GRETHE IS A VERY ENTHUSIASTIC READER!

Followed by the big night...
THANK YOU ALL FOR COMING, I HOPE YOU ENJOY YOUR STAY IN ARENDELLE!
I'M CERTAIN WE WILL, QUEEN ELSA. YOUR SPEECH WAS QUITE PERSUASIVE!

I'D CALL THAT A SUCCESSFUL DAY. THE CHILDREN WERE THRILLED, AND THE DELEGATES SEEM HAPPY...
BECAUSE I REMEMBERED TO DELEGATE! AND NOW I'M REALLY LOOKING FORWARD TO...

...A GOOD NIGHT'S SLEEP!

The End

UNEXPECTED FINALE

Manuscript: Tea Orsi; Layout: Alberto Zanon; Cleanup: Letizia Algeri; Color: MichelAngela World

The End

A Snowgie-Hug

ANNA'S PLANNED A SURPRISE FOR HER SISTER...

OKAY EVERYONE, HERE'S THE **PLAN**...

ALL YOU NEED TO DO IS TO **REMEMBER** YOUR PLACE IN THE **SNOWFLAKE**!

LET'S **START** NOW! ELSA WILL BE HERE SOON!

Manuscript: Tea Orsi; Layout: Alberto Zanon; Cleanup: Letizia Algeri; Color: Dario Calabria

SLUSH AND FLURRY YOU CAN COMPLETE THIS PART! WELL DONE, SLUDGE!

GOOD IDEA, ANSEL AND POWDER! THAT ADDS A **SPECIAL EFFECT**!
POING
POING

AND...
THAT'S AMAZING! ELSA WILL LOVE THIS **HUGE SNOWGIE-FLAKE**!

GOOD JOB! YOU CAN TAKE A BREAK. BUT WHEN SHE GETS HERE, IT'S SHOWTIME!

JUST THEN...
HI THERE! I GOT HERE A BIT EARLY. NOW, WHAT DID YOU WANT TO SHOW ME?

PSSST! TAKE YOUR PLACES!

HUH?!? WHAT A GREAT WELCOME!
WELL... THERE'S REALLY NOTHING BETTER THAN A BIG SNOWGIE HUG!
POING
POING
POING
POING
POING
POING

The End

Disney

CLASSIC STORIES RETOLD
WITH THE MAGIC OF DISNEY!

DISNEY TREASURE ISLAND, starring Mickey Mouse

Robert Louis Stevenson's classic tale of pirates, treasure, and swashbuckling adventure comes to life in this adaptation!

978-1-50671-158-4 ✠ $10.99

DISNEY DON QUIXOTE, starring Goofy & Mickey Mouse

A knight-errant and the power of his imagination finds reality in this adaptation of the classic by Miguel de Cervantes!

978-1-50671-216-1 ✠ $10.99

DISNEY MOBY DICK, starring Donald Duck

In an adaptation of Herman Melville's classic, sailors venture out on the high seas in pursuit of the white whale Moby Dick.

978-1-50671-157-7 ✠ $10.99

DISNEY DRACULA, starring Mickey Mouse

Enter a world where vampires rise up from the shadows in this adaptation of Bram Stoker's classic horror!

978-1-50671-217-8 ✠ $10.99

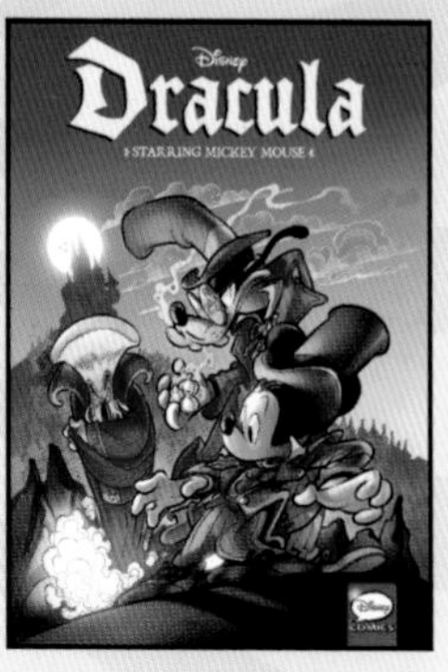

DISNEY HAMLET, starring Donald Duck

The ghost of a betrayed king appoints Prince Ducklet to restore peace to his kingdom in this adaptation of William Shakespeare's tragedy.

978-1-50671-219-2 ✠ $10.99

DISNEY FRANKENSTEIN, starring Donald Duck

An electrifying adaptation of the classic novel by Mary Shelley exploring themes of nature and fate!

978-1-50671-218-5 ✠ $10.99

AVAILABLE AT YOUR LOCAL COMICS SHOP OR BOOKSTORE!
To find a comics shop in your area, visit comicshoplocator.com. For more information or to order direct, visit DarkHorse.com

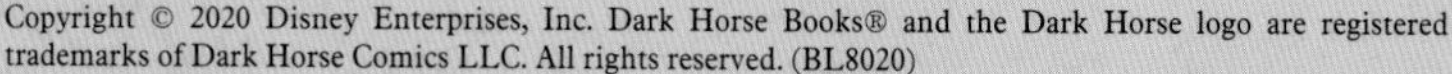